She wasn't about to let him get away...

Before Lani could get her bearings, her assailant punched her and pushed her back off the side of the boat. She splashed into the water, plunging beneath the surface as the boat sped out into open water.

Feeling defeated, she turned and swam back toward the beach. Noah rushed out into the water up to his knees. She gasped for air.

"You all right?" He wrapped his arm around her and helped her to the beach.

The suspect had gotten away.

She stared out where the flashing light of the assailant's boat merged with other flashing lights.

If a training exercise could go so far off the rails, what would happen when she worked the field?

TRUE BLUE K-9 UNIT:

These police officers fight for justice
with the help of their brave canine partners.

Ever since she found the Nancy Drew books with the pink covers in her country school library, **Sharon Dunn** has loved mystery and suspense. Most of her books take place in Montana, where she lives with three nearly grown children and a hyper border collie. She lost her beloved husband of twenty-seven years to cancer in 2014. When she isn't writing, she loves to hike surrounded by God's beauty.

Books by Sharon Dunn

Love Inspired Suspense

True Blue K-9 Unit
Courage Under Fire

Dead Ringer
Night Prey
Her Guardian
Broken Trust
Zero Visibility
Montana Standoff
Top Secret Identity
Wilderness Target
Cold Case Justice
Mistaken Target
Fatal Vendetta
Big Sky Showdown
Hidden Away
In Too Deep
Wilderness Secrets

Texas Ranger Holidays
Thanksgiving Protector

COURAGE
UNDER FIRE

SHARON DUNN

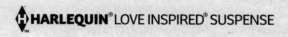

HARLEQUIN® LOVE INSPIRED® SUSPENSE

Special thanks and acknowledgment are given to Sharon Dunn for her contribution to the True Blue K-9 Unit miniseries.

Recycling programs
for this product may
not exist in your area.

LOVE INSPIRED BOOKS

ISBN-13: 978-1-335-23237-3

Courage Under Fire

www.Harlequin.com

Printed in U.S.A.

Be of good courage, and he shall strengthen your heart,
all ye that hope in the Lord.
—*Psalm* 31:24

For the dog who saved my life and is
my writing companion, Bart the hyper border collie.

ONE

Rookie K-9 officer Lani Branson took in a deep breath as she pedaled her bike along the trail in the Jamaica Bay Wildlife Refuge. She could hear birds chattering. Water rushed and receded from the shore just over the dunes. The high-rises of New York City, made hazy from the dusky twilight, were visible across the expanse of water.

She sped up even more.

Tonight was important. This training exercise was an opportunity to prove herself to the other K-9 officers who waited back at the visitors' center with the tracking dogs for her to give the go-ahead. Playing the part of a child lost in the refuge so the dogs could practice tracking her was probably a less than desirable duty for the senior officers. As a new recruit to the NYC K-9 Command Unit, she understood the pecking order. If she did a good job tonight, she'd be given more responsibility.

Though she was in solid shape, her leg muscles strained as she willed herself to pedal even faster. The trail ended. She pushed her bike into a hiding place in the brush and headed toward the tall grass that surrounded the shore. A flock of birds took to the air. Their squawking and flapping of wings filled the gray sky. Her heart beat a little faster. God's creation never ceased to amaze her.

She stuttered in her step, squinting to make out details in the early evening light. She wondered what had alarmed the birds. Though people might be around the surrounding area, the rangers had secured this part of the refuge for the training exercise. That didn't mean someone curious about what the NYPD was up to hadn't snuck into the area. Could be anything or nothing at all, sometimes birds just decided to fly away.

She ran through the tall grass that bordered the salt marsh and then toward the open area of the dunes. She needed to get far enough away for it to be a challenge for the dogs to find her.

As a sense of unease invaded her awareness, she stopped. She had felt on edge for the last few days. A car had tailed her through traffic just this morning and more than once she'd felt the press of a gaze on her only to turn and see no one.

Reaching up to her shoulder, Lani pressed the button on the radio. "I'm in place."

The smooth tenor voice of her supervisor, Chief Noah Jameson, came over the line. "Good, you made it out there in record time."

As she hurried steadily toward the tall brush, Lani had an extra bounce in her step. Since her training as a K-9 officer had begun, that was the first compliment Noah had given her. Noah had been appointed the interim chief of the NYC K-9 Command Unit after the untimely death of his brother Jordan—the former chief. A permanent replacement was yet to be named.

Noah's voice floated over the radio. "Remember, move like a five-year-old would."

"Ten-four." In fact, Noah always seemed to be quite tight-lipped whenever she was around. He had a great deal on his mind. Jordan had been murdered months ago and the investigation had stalled. All the same, Noah seemed to be extra quiet around her. She took his silence to be disapproval. Maybe like some of the other officers, he didn't think she was up to the job.

Lani was a natural athlete with a background as a self-defense instructor and a dancer. She'd graduated from the academy with flying colors and she had an older brother, Reed, who was also with the unit. It was her former profession as an actress that probably made them wonder if she would make the cut. All officers earned a nickname sooner or later. Hers was less than flattering. They called her Cover Girl. Never mind that she'd never worked as a model. She was stuck with the name…for now. Lani gritted her teeth. The rest of the team just didn't know what she was made of.

She entered a grove of trees. The dry autumn leaves crackled as the breeze rushed over them. It could be up to an hour before the dogs found her. The refuge was thousands of acres. The places a child could get lost were infinite. She passed a wooden box on a stake. A barn owl peeked out of the round hole in the box. Jamaica Bay was home to hundreds of species of birds. This time of year, the raptors showed up.

Lani was New York City born and bred. One of her favorite memories was of her grandfather taking her to see the eagles.

Knowing that a child would not move in a logical way, she headed back toward the shore and ran along the beach for a while before zigzagging back into the brush. Her heart pounded in her chest. Though she still had her radio, her instructions were not to communicate with the rest of the team.

Up ahead she spotted an object shining in the setting sun. She jogged toward it. A bicycle, not hers, was propped against a tree.

A knot of tension formed at the back of her neck as she turned a half circle, taking in the area around her. It was possible someone had left the bike behind. Vagrants could have wandered into the area.

She studied the bike a little closer. State-of-the-art and in good condition. Not the kind of bike someone just dumped.

Still puzzled by her find, Lani hurried deeper into the trees and then sat down on the ground. A five-year-old would stop and rest, she reasoned, maybe even fall asleep. She stared at the sky.

The noisy chatter of the gulls and other birds feeding hummed in the background. Wind rustled the leaves, some of them already golden and red, others still green, creating a sort of song.

She listened, thinking she might hear the baying of the dogs as they picked up her scent and tracked her. No. It was too soon for that. Though it would have been a welcome sound.

A branch cracked. Her breath caught in her throat. To the best of her knowledge, there were no large animals on the refuge, only squirrels, rodents and raccoons. Fear caused her heartbeat to drum in her ears. She touched the radio on her shoulder.

More noise landed on her ears. Whatever was in the thick brush that surrounded her was on the move.

She took her hand off the radio, shaking her head. It would not go over big for her to push the panic button over some nocturnal creature looking for its dinner.

Lani rose to her feet and headed toward the tall grass where she would lie down as though she'd fallen asleep. The dogs and their handlers needed to read the signs she left behind. Her feet pounded the hard-packed ground as she turned back to the shore. The cacophony of the birds feeding by the water's edge grew louder.

Out of the corner of her eye, she caught movement, a bright color. Human? The rest of the team couldn't have found her that fast.

"NYPD." She hadn't worn her gun for this exercise. Her eyes scanned all around her, searching for movement and color. "You need to show yourself."

Seconds ticked by. Her heart pounded.

Someone else was out here.

Again, it was possible that a junkie or vagrant had found a way to avoid detection and was making the refuge his or her home.

The birds quieted as the sun slipped lower in the sky. All she heard was the sound of her own heartbeat. Her hand moved to the radio. She needed to at least inform Noah that someone else was lurking in the bushes. She clicked the radio on and turned her head to speak into it.

A hand slapped hers and yanked the radio off her shoulder. Automatically, she reacted with an elbow punch to her assailant's stomach.

Her attacker groaned in pain but did not relent in his attack. He restrained her by locking her neck in the crook of his elbow while he pulled her arm behind her and pushed it up at a painful angle with his other hand.

The fear that invaded every cell of her body was

overridden by her years of training in self-defense. She kicked him hard in the shin. His grip didn't loosen at all. The man was strong and had a high tolerance for pain.

He held on tight, dragging her toward the tall grass and the water. Her arm burned from pain as he bent it behind her back and pushed it upward.

She planted her feet.

Her resistance seemed to fuel his anger. He squeezed her neck tighter.

She struggled for air. She kicked him several times even as dots formed in her field of vision. He jerked back and up with his crooked arm. She landed one more intense blow to his leg.

His grip loosened enough for her to twist free. She ran only a few steps before he grabbed her shirt and dragged her back toward him. She spun around landing a chop to his neck designed to cause pain by pinching nerves. The move disabled her attacker long enough for her to get a head start.

The ground was softer this close to the shore. The water of the bay shimmered in her peripheral vision as she sprinted. She needed to get back up to the trail to find her bike before he could grab her again.

The landscape darkened and shadows covered the trees and bushes as the last light of the sun faded. His footsteps pounded behind her. She willed herself to go faster. Air filled her lungs and her breathing intensified. She veered off, hoping to head back up toward the trail and her bike.

She attacker remained close at her heels. Just as she arrived at her bike, he grabbed her. She whirled around, getting in several solid blows. He grabbed her by the shoulders and spun her around.

The attacker wrapped his arms around her, coming at her from behind. He seemed to want to restrain her rather than fight back. His arms suctioned around her like an anaconda. His mouth was very close to her ear.

"There now," he said.

His warm breath and sickly sweet words sent a new wave of fear through her. When she tried to twist free, he tightened his grip on her waist.

Then she heard a most welcome sound, the dogs baying and barking. Still some distance away but clearly headed toward her.

The man let go of her and stepped back. He wore a hat and she could not see his face in the dim light. Clearly frightened by the approaching dogs, he turned to go. She wasn't about to let him get away. She leaped through the air, seeking to knock him to the ground. The attacker did not fall, which left her hanging on to his back.

"NYPD," she shouted.

He shook her off, ran a few paces and then bent over.

She caught up with him. He swung around. In the darkness, she had not seen him pick up the rock he now had in his hand. It hit the side of her head. Her knees buckled.

The ground drew ever closer as dots filled her field of vision.

Her attacker loomed above her. "Next time."

She heard his retreating footsteps as her world went black.

Noah Jameson's heartbeat ticked up a notch as he let his Rottweiler, Scotty, pick up the scent of Officer Lani Branson. Three dogs on their long leads sniffed, barked and circled back to spots before taking off on the trail. Officer Finn Gallagher's K-9 partner, a yellow Lab trained in search and rescue, took the lead. Reed Branson, Lani's brother, followed with bloodhound Jessie, a tracking K-9.

The dogs' enthusiasm was infectious. This kind of excitement made him feel alive. This was what he loved about police work, the action. Being out in the field nourished him even if it was just a training exercise. It beat sitting behind a desk putting out administrative fires and keeping the upper brass happy.

Until his murder last spring, Noah's older brother Jordan had been the chief of the NYC K-9 Command Unit. Though there had been some jockeying for the job, Noah had been the one appointed to fill his brother's shoes, temporarily at least. He missed working the street with Scotty, chasing down leads and suspects. More than anything, he missed his older brother. That the NYPD, himself included, had been unable to track down Jordan's killer only made the wound more raw and the grief harder to bear.

Scotty kept his nose to the ground as they worked their way along the path. Scotty was trained in emergency services which meant he could do a little of everything. The other dogs kept pace with Scotty.

So far the trail had been easy enough to follow, but they hadn't found Lani's bicycle yet. Once she got off the bike, she'd been instructed to move in the same erratic pattern a five-year-old might take. Though he had his concerns about Lani's ability to be a K-9 officer, she had a good attitude about being the guinea pig.

A tightening in his chest indicated his doubts were getting the better of him. Once she was in place, Lani was to have no communication with him or anyone on the team. He thought he'd heard the radio turn on and then off suddenly. It was probably nothing. Lani was in great physical condition and had done well at the academy, it was just that her chattiness made her come across as lacking confidence. Anytime he had interacted with her, Lani tended to talk a mile a minute.

The sky darkened as they headed up the trail. Noah and the other officers jogged to keep up with the dogs. They worked their way on the path running for at least twenty minutes. The dogs stopped and split off the trail, each of them alerting and then sniffing in a circle. This must be where Lani had left the trail.

Noah followed Scotty through the tangled brush.

"Come on, boy, you can find her."

Scotty raised his head, sniffed the air and then put his nose back on the ground. He picked up the scent again. They headed off the trail into the tall grass. Scotty lifted his head and sat on his back haunches. That was his hard alert. Noah stared into the brush. Metal shone in the waning light.

He'd found the bicycle.

Noah spoke into his radio. "Scotty's picked up the trail."

The two other dogs bayed and fell in behind Scotty. The dogs took them across the dunes back into the trees and down to the shore. Though he could still hear the barking, the dogs spread out as they moved through the trees.

Reed's panic-filled voice came across the line. "We got a problem. You better come see this."

Noah could see Reed and Jessie through the tangle of brush. Judging from the high-pitched baying, Jessie was excited. No sign of Lani. He shortened the lead on Scotty and hurried through the trees.

"What is it?"

Reed held up a police radio. Lani's. Reed's voice filled with concern. "She wouldn't tear it off herself. Something's gone wrong."

There was only a small chance the radio had gotten hung up on something as she ran. Noah's thoughts raced as he took in the scene around him. Both dogs indicated a high level of excitement. The grass was smashed down. Some sort of struggle had taken place.

"The dogs will find her. If someone else is out here too, we'll find him as well."

Noah radioed the other handler, Finn, to see if his Lab picked up on any new scent.

As they followed the dogs through the brush, Noah pushed away any negative thoughts. If he'd learned anything from his K-9 partner, it was to stay focused.

Reed and Jessie headed in a different direction, maybe toward whomever else was out here.

Scotty worked methodically. Jessie sniffed a different area, more toward the shore, trying to find the trail. A new level of panic invaded Noah's awareness as Scotty worked his way through the brush and then sat down, head held high.

Noah saw Lani's blond hair visible in the moonlight. Her motionless body twisted at an odd angle set off alarm bells as he hurried toward her.

He drew close and kneeled beside her. Scotty emitted a whine and then leaned to lick Lani's face. Still, she did not move.

"I'm worried too," said Noah. As he gazed at her motionless body, the grief over the loss of his brother hit him like a semitruck. Another officer wasn't going to die, not on his watch. His fingers touched Lani's neck. Her pulse pushed back on his fingertips. He breathed a sigh of relief. She was still alive. There was a bruise on the side of her head. Her hair had worked loose of the tight bun she kept it in when on duty. Signs that she'd been in a fight.

While Noah radioed for medical help, Reed rushed toward them through the tangle of brush.

He let out a groan as he knelt beside his sister.

Lani's eyes fluttered open, and she lifted her head and shoulders. On impulse, he gathered her into his arms.

"She's alive," said Noah. His voice filled with elation. "We need to call for backup. Get some more searchers to the refuge. Someone attacked Lani and we need to find him before he escapes."

TWO

Lani stared into Noah's calm face. He'd wrapped his arm around her back holding her up as he kneeled and faced her.

In the waning light, she could just make out the tiniest of smiles. "Hey. Good to see you coming around." His voice held a note of joy. Normally very stoic, it was the first time she had seen any emotion at all from Noah.

"Hey, sis." Reed's voice drew her attention as he kneeled off to the side. Jessie lay down beside him. The bloodhound's big floppy ears touched the ground.

Scotty leaned in and licked her face.

The Rottweiler's affectionate response stirred her into full consciousness. "Whoa, what a greeting." She sat up rubbing Scotty's barrel chest and nuzzling her face against his.

Both Reed and Noah laughed at Scotty.

Petting the dog behind the ears, Lani pulled away from Noah. Silence fell between the three of them. Her breath caught as the memory of the attack invaded her thoughts, breaking the moment of levity.

Reed spoke up. "You all right?"

"My head hurts," she said. It was easier to think about her physical pain. She touched the sore spot where the rock had hit her.

Noah cleared his throat. "What happened?" He pulled back and squared his shoulders, returning to his old professional self. So much for the small sign that Noah Jameson was human.

Heat rose up in her cheeks. Now she would have to explain why the training exercise had gone sideways. She still didn't know who the man was or why he had come after her. She hadn't even gotten a good look at him. She leaned forward to get to her feet but sat back down. Pain shot through the side of her head. "Ouch." Scotty edged in close to her, emitting a whine that suggested deep concern.

Reed leaned a little closer as well. "Take it easy."

Noah repeated his question. "What happened? There was someone else out here. Who was he?"

The memory of that man talking into her ear, of not being able to subdue him, hit her full force. "Yes, I was attacked." Her voice faltered, but she took in a breath and regained her composure. The last thing she wanted was for Noah to think she couldn't handle herself.

Scotty licked her cheek. Reed put a hand on her shoulder.

Noah rose to his feet. "I thought that might be the case. We've got reinforcements coming in to search the area."

"Did you see the guy?" Reed rose to his feet.

"No, it was dark. We struggled." She glanced nervously at Noah. His expression gave nothing away. "I can give a full statement as to what happened. The guy was in good shape. I found a bike that might be his."

She gave them a summary of the attack but then kept talking. Lani bit her lip. She was rambling because Noah's silence made her nervous. "We should try to locate that. It might be his means of escape. Certainly, it might have fingerprints or other evidence." Why was she talking like it was going out of style?

"We'll start searching before the others get here. Time is precious." Noah had already signaled Scotty to stand beside him.

"I'll help with the search. I can at least lead you to where I saw the bicycle." She moved to get to her feet.

"You've had physical trauma. Maybe you should stay put," said Reed.

Reed had shown considerable restraint. She could tell from his expression he was worried. He knew when they were out in the field, she wanted to be treated like a fellow officer not the little sister.

"I'll be fine." She stood up. Already she could feel the bruising and strained muscles from the fight she'd been in, but she wasn't about to let Noah know that. "I can show where I found the bike, maybe the dogs can pick up a scent."

Noah nodded. He pulled his flashlight off his belt and handed it to her. "If you are fine with that. Lead the way."

Lani took the flashlight. Was that approval she heard in his voice? In all other settings, she was a confident person. She had a black belt and good instincts. Why did she always second-guess herself around Noah?

With Reed, Noah and the dogs following, Lani made her way back to where she remembered seeing the bicycle. She saw the tree where the bike had been propped. Of course, it was gone. The man must have taken off on it.

"Right here. It was right here." She shone the light all around.

The dogs circled giving a soft alert to some sort of smell.

She saw the most likely path the bike could have gone on. The dogs picked up the scent and headed in that direction. The sky had become black with the city skyline glittering in the distance. Always a beautiful sight. She loved the city at night.

The brush grew denser as they got closer to the shore. She saw a flash of light up ahead. The dogs barked and bayed excitedly. That had to be her attacker.

Lani ran, following the light as it winked in and out of view and then disappeared close to the shore. The light must be on the attacker's bicycle.

She ran faster despite the terrain becoming more treacherous and the pain from her injuries. With Reed and Noah right behind her, she made her way down the steep incline. The faint silhouette of a boat was visible in the moonlight. She heard a motor roar to life. The man had loaded his bike into the boat and was preparing to take off.

She wasn't about to let him get away.

The boat had just eased away from the shore when she jumped into the water. In the distance, she could see the flashing lights of other boats.

This boat wouldn't be able to get up speed until it was in open water out of the bay and the tangle of peninsulas and islands that made up the refuge.

Her arms cut through the surging waves. Her head bobbed above the surface. She was within feet of the boat. She willed herself to move faster. Her hand reached for the edge of the boat. She held on.

She could see the back of the man as he steered. The bike occupied two of the backseats. She pulled herself up. Water cascaded off her body. The noise was enough to alert her assailant. He shifted the boat into Neutral and whirled around.

Before she could get her bearings, he had punched her and pushed her back off the side of the boat. She splashed into the water, plunging beneath the surface like a weighted rag doll. She bobbed back up just in time to see the boat speeding out into open water.

She could hear the dogs on the shore going ballistic. Feeling defeated, she turned and swam back toward the beach. Noah rushed out into the water up to his knees. She gasped for air.

"You all right?" He wrapped his arm around her and helped her to the beach.

The suspect had gotten away. Noah eased her down to the beach where Scotty waited to give her moral support and doggie kisses. The cold water had masked the pain of her attack. Now she could feel where there was probably going to be some soreness and bruising.

She stared out where the flashing light of the assailant's boat merged with other flashing lights. Not many boats out at this hour. "Maybe the coast guard can catch up with him." She didn't hold out much hope for that happening.

Noah spoke on his radio, giving a description of the boat and the direction it was headed.

Noah sat down beside her. "That was something else, jumping in the water like that."

That Noah was impressed with her was only a small victory. The suspect had gotten away. She was exhausted, beat and wondering if she had made the right choice following in her brother's footsteps.

Her only consolation was that Scotty seemed to pick up on her despair. The Rottweiler rested his chin on her leg and made a sympathetic noise. Now she remembered why she wanted to be a K-9 cop. She rested a hand on Scotty's head. Someday she would be assigned her own K-9 partner.

Tonight though, she felt defeated. If a training exercise could go so far off the rails, what would happen when she worked the field?

Noah sat beside Lani, catching his breath. "Maybe they'll nab him when he comes to shore."

The other dogs and officers were farther inland.

"Maybe." Lani's voice sounded weak. She stroked behind Scotty's ears.

Noah's Rottweiler usually didn't warm up to people so fast, but the dog seemed to like Lani from the moment she'd become a part of the K-9 unit. His brother Jordan had always said that dogs were a good judge of character. If he closed his eyes, he could almost hear his brother's voice. He rubbed his chest though the pain he felt was emotional, that deep chasm inside that would never be filled. His younger brothers Zach and Carter were probably the only two people who understood about the hole Jordan's death had left for all of them. His parents were going through a whole different kind of grief.

"I appreciate your tenacity in going after the suspect," he said. Noah remembered that only a month before, Lani had stopped an intruder in her and Reed's house by shooting him. Though she had handled herself well, she had been put on administrative leave to help with her emotional recovery, which had stalled her training. Remembering that and seeing firsthand how she had done tonight made Noah think that maybe he had underestimated Lani.

Lani wrapped her arms around her body. "He got away though."

Noah took off his jacket and wrapped it around her shoulders. His pants were wet up to the knees, but he wasn't cold. "If medical hasn't shown up yet at the visitors' center, let's get you checked out in the ER."

She drew the coat around her. "I'm fine. I just need to change into some dry clothes and get some rest."

"You took quite a blow to the head." Though Lani seemed like a strong woman, he was concerned about the psychological fallout from having been attacked tonight in addition to her physical well-being. Sometimes there was an accumulative effect from dealing with violence and then an officer just cracked up.

"I know about the possibility of a concussion. Reed gets off duty in a bit, he can keep an eye on me through the night. As soon as that suspect is picked up, I want to be called. I don't care what the hour is."

"Sure, Lani." Always at the back of his mind, the fear of something bad happening to another of the K-9 officers plagued him. He felt a strong responsibility to the team. "At least ride home with me in my patrol car."

He rose to his feet and held out his hand to help her up. Her fingers felt silky soft in his calloused bear paws. They stood for a moment facing each other. The rhythm of water rushing the shore and the gulls feeding in the distance seemed to be the only sounds.

"Fine, I'll ride back with you, but I will report for duty for my regular shift tomorrow. Don't treat me with kid gloves." Lani turned and headed up the sandy shore toward the tall grass. "I can handle myself just fine. I've had first aid training as part of being a martial arts instructor..."

Lani continued to talk as they moved through the grass.

He wasn't sure if her talking was a sign of confidence or insecurity. His estimation of her had gone up a notch. It took guts to jump in the water after a suspect, especially one that had just attacked her.

Noah's radio glitched and Reed's voice came across the line. "I got Lani's bike loaded up in my patrol car."

"Ten-four. She's riding home with me, but you need to keep an eye on her through the night."

"She's not going into the ER?" Reed's voice filled with concern.

Lani grabbed the radio. Standing on her tiptoes, she spoke into it. "Reed, quit being a big brother. When we're working, treat me like you would any other officer."

"Copy that, sis."

"Do you call all the other officers, sis?"

Noah chuckled at the banter between the siblings. His brothers razzed each other and him on and off the job.

"Yes, Officer Branson." Reed's voice held a note of amusement.

Lani addressed Noah. "We'll swing by the ER, but I'm sure I'm fine," Lani said.

They hiked back up to the trail and out to the visitors' center. Several patrol cars were parked there. More had arrived once the alert about the suspect had gone out.

"Any news on the boat?" Lani stepped toward one of the other officers, who shook his head.

Noah loaded Scotty in the back of his Tahoe SUV.

Lani got into the passenger seat. They pulled out of the visitors' center. Noah veered toward Cross Bay Boulevard, Lani doing most of the talking sharing about the kids' class she taught at the martial arts center.

They stopped in the ER where a doctor examined Lani and gave her the okay to go back to work after a day off, but cautioned her to watch for any pain or loss of focus for the next couple of days. They got back into the Tahoe and headed home. Lani continued to talk about working with dogs at the training center.

As they drove through Queens at night, her voice trailed off. She touched her hand to her shoulder.

He'd gotten so used to the sound of her voice, the silence felt awkward. He glanced over at her. "Everything okay, Lani?"

"My radio. He yanked it off of me. I don't have a radio anymore." Her voice, normally very animated, had become monotone.

Noah had been braced for the emotional shock to set in. "We'll issue you a new one when you come on shift after your day of rest. Lani?"

He was only a few blocks from her house in Rego Park. Lani and Reed lived on a quiet street. At this hour, there was no one outside. He spoke again to get her attention. "Lani?"

"I'm all right." She stared straight ahead.

He knew she wasn't. "It's pretty normal to feel off-kilter after what you've been through." She hadn't been an officer very long and already she'd seen a degree of violence. "It wouldn't hurt to make an appointment with the police psychologist. I know it was required you meet with one after you shot that guy who came into your house. It wouldn't hurt to make another appointment."

She lifted her chin slightly. "I just need a good night's sleep and run in the park in the morning. That's my therapy."

He had a feeling the bravado she showed was because she didn't want to appear incapable in front of the chief. Sometimes he didn't like his title. It put a barrier between him and his fellow officers.

After circling the block, he found a parking space not too far from her house. He appreciated how tough she was acting. He'd been a cop long enough to know that denial didn't make the trauma go away. "At least let me stay with you until Reed gets off shift."

She lowered her head and pushed open the car door. "Okay, but only if Scotty can come in too."

Scotty let out a low-level woof of approval.

Both of them laughed.

"Scotty seems to like the idea," said Lani.

He had to hand it to his square-jawed partner. He could be very entertaining. Noah walked Lani to the house which had a stone facade and pillars. The flower beds were covered in straw. Though he could picture them in full bloom. Lani struck him as a plant kind of person. Who was he kidding? Lani was a people person and a dog person—warm and connecting, vivacious about all aspects of life. That's why it bothered him to see her so quiet.

With Scotty heeling beside him, they went up the steps and onto the porch. Lani unlocked the door.

Noah stared up at the second story. "This whole place is yours?"

"No, we have an upstairs tenant." She pushed the door open.

Once inside, Lani invited Noah to sit on the couch

while Scotty sniffed his new surroundings. She excused herself to change out of her wet clothes.

Family photos, many of Reed and Lani doing sports together, adorned the wall in the living room. There was a picture of them attending a Yankees game with an older couple. Judging from the resemblance, the older couple must be Reed and Lani's parents. His eyes rested on a picture of a teenage Lani in a leotard with her arms around two other dancers. A more recent one showed Lani on stage in a Western costume with other actors.

Noah understood why Lani was referred to as Cover Girl by the rest of the team. Her vitality and positive attitude came across in the photos and she was beautiful enough to be a model.

Several photos featured Reed working with his K-9 partner, Jessie.

Lani entered the room dressed in an oversize orange sweatshirt and jeans. "Do you want some cocoa or something?" Her blue eyes did not have their usual sparkle. He detected the weariness in her voice. It was important that she not be alone after having gone through such an ordeal.

"Sure, that sounds good," he said. "Let me help you."

While Lani filled the kettle and put it on the stove, Noah rooted through cupboards for mugs.

Lani pulled a basket filled with tea bags and hot chocolate packets from a cupboard. "Pick whatever you like."

The toll of the attack was evident in her movement and on her face. He placed a hand on her shoulder. "Why don't you go sit down and I'll bring you the drink?"

She nodded and stepped back into the living room.

Again, he knew something was up because she didn't argue with him.

He opened the packets of cocoa and sprinkled them into the mugs. The kettle whistled. He poured the water into the cups. He carried the steaming mugs into the living room where he found Lani standing, not sitting, staring at the wall of photographs. Scotty had finished sniffing his surroundings and now sat at attention. His ears perked up when Noah entered the room.

She pointed to a bare space on the wall. "Do you know what goes there?"

Noah shook his head.

"A picture of me with my dog when I'm assigned one." Her face shone with a sort of inner glow.

The bare space was next to a photo of Reed with his Jessie. The bloodhound's saggy-skinned expression seemed to contradict the dog's tenacious personality.

He knew from Lani's file that she was twenty-nine, old for a rookie. His estimation of her abilities had changed, but he still had his doubts. Her background was not the normal career route for a cop. "That will happen soon enough." It had been months since Lani had been accepted to the K-9 unit and a suitable dog had still not become available. She'd tried out several. The dogs were either not compatible with her or they washed out of the program. Jordan's death and Noah getting used to being chief had slowed everything down as well.

"Tonight didn't go like I expected." She stared at the floor.

He stepped toward her, touching her chin so she lifted her eyes. "But you handled the unexpected. That's what a good cop does."

A little light came into her blue eyes. That spark of energy that he liked about her returned.

"Thanks," she said.

She let out a heavy breath and sat down on the couch. Noah sat down beside her sipping his beverage. Scotty lay down so his butt rested against Noah's feet and his head rested close to Lani's feet.

Noah pointed toward the photos. "So you did a lot of plays?" It was important to keep her mind off the attack.

"Mostly off Broadway, and I did a couple commercials and even some stunt work," she said.

"I know I've lived here my whole life, but I think I made it to the theater twice in my life and one time it was with my school."

Lani laughed, "I know. There are people born and raised here who have never been to the Statue of Liberty."

He reached down to pat Scotty's head. "My family goes to the Mets games quite a bit."

"Sounds like fun." Lani took a sip of her cocoa.

They talked awhile longer. When the door opened and Reed stepped in with Jessie, Noah glanced at the clock. An hour had passed without him realizing he'd been so caught up in his conversation with Lani.

Jessie loped over to Lani, who leaned so the dog could give her a sloppy kiss.

"Long night?"

"Something like that. Had a couple other calls after we got stuff wrapped up at the refuge." Reed took his coat off and hung it up on a coatrack. "Sorry I'm late. I stopped in to talk with Abigail for a little bit."

Abigail was Reed's fiancée and an outreach coordinator for troubled teens.

"Can I talk to you for just a moment?" Noah gestured for Reed to enter the kitchen.

"What's up?"

"Keep an eye on her through the night. Not just to make sure she doesn't lose consciousness. Wake her up a couple of times. The ER doc said to look for dilated pupils. I'm more worried about her emotional health. Maybe she's just acting tough in front of me. I don't know."

Reed nodded. "We got this handled. I know my sister."

"She'll push to come into work tomorrow, but she needs to take the day off," said Noah.

Reed nodded. "Will do."

When they returned to the living room, Lani had fallen asleep on the couch. Jessie curled against her belly. The bloodhound was so huge she hung halfway off the couch. Lani's blond hair, loose from the tight bun, framed her face and fell across her neck.

Scotty lay at Lani's feet. He stared up at Noah while his tail thudded on the floor.

Noah commanded Scotty to come and he fell in line. "I'll see myself out." He glanced once again at the sleeping Lani. She looked at peace. "Take care of her. Maybe you can talk her into making a counseling appointment."

"You can't talk my sister into anything once she's made up her mind."

"So true." Noah stepped to the door, swung it open and headed up the block toward his SUV with the dog padding softly on the sidewalk beside him. He looked back. The curtains were drawn in the living room. Still, he could picture Reed placing a blanket over his sleeping sister. She was in good hands.

As he loaded Scotty into the patrol car, he felt that tightening in his chest.

He only hoped that what had happened to Lani tonight was an isolated incident. He didn't want another cop harmed…or worse.

THREE

Lani clicked the leash onto the collar of the six-month-old yellow Lab and headed out of the training center to walk the pup. She was glad to be back to work after a required day off. Oscar was one of eight puppies born to Stella, a yellow Lab, who had been a gift to the unit from the Czech Republic. The dogs had all been put into foster homes. Oscar had been brought back to the training center to assess if he would be good K-9 material and maybe assigned to Lani. She tried not to get too hopeful about Oscar. Other dogs she'd trained with had initially seemed like a good fit. She pushed aside the frustration she felt over not getting her own K-9 partner after so many months.

As she stepped out into the early morning to walk the dog, the sun bathed her skin. She turned the corner.

The idea of taking the dogs out was not only for exercise but getting them used to staying focused with a million distractions around them. This street usually had fewer people and less traffic than Ninety-Fourth Street where the K-9 offices and training center were.

All the same, the streets already bustled with activity, visual and auditory. Oscar heeled with his head up, taking in the buzz of the city. Pedestrians brushed past them on the sidewalks. Car horns blared as traffic rolled by. In the distance, she detected the intense rhythm of a jackhammer.

This was her city. Walking the dogs was part of her routine while on duty. Still, a fearful hesitation made her a little less confident in her step. The boat her attacker had escaped in was never found. She'd gone for a run on her day off which usually cleared her head, but not this time. Her sleep had been fitful.

Oscar's tail wagged when a group of children walked past him. She gave the leash a slight jerk to let him know that as much as he wanted to, he couldn't interact with the children.

"We're on duty," she said.

The crowd thinned as they approached an abandoned building that used to be a multistoried department store. She could feel the soreness from the attack. She increased her pace. Oscar's little legs kept up with hers. If she slowed, he responded. The dog was sharp. She loved all the K-9 recruits, but she liked how quickly Oscar picked up on her cues. They seemed to be dialed into each other, a quality that was essential in working with a partner, K-9 or human.

She'd requested that he be brought out of foster care to see if he'd be good K-9 material. Not all dogs had the temperament to be K-9s. In her first encounter with Oscar, when he was just weaned at eight weeks, he had sat back on his haunches and looked up at her, tilting his head to one side as if to say, *At your service, ma'am*.

Oscar seemed to have alerted on something across the street. She followed the line of his gaze. Noah Jameson stood beside a coffee cart waiting for his morning cup. He offered Lani a small wave before he turned back toward headquarters. He must be busy today if he was getting his coffee from a street cart. Most of the officers went to Griffin's diner for coffee. Scotty wasn't with him. He must be back at Noah's office.

"He's all right, isn't he, Oscar?" Noah had always struck her as being emotionally closed down. She had seen a more caring side to him after the training exercise fell apart. Maybe he was human after all.

A scraping sound above her caused her to tilt her head. A large square object came right toward her at a rapid speed, filling her field of vision. She jumped to one side, falling against the brick exterior of the building. The few people on the sidewalk scattered as well. In her panic, Lani had let go of Oscar's leash.

An air-conditioning unit shattered on the concrete. Some of the pieces still vibrated from the impact.

An older man rushed toward her. "Are you all right?"

Dazed and in shock, Lani got to her feet with the man's help. She brushed the dust off her uniform.

"What a bizarre accident." An older woman approached Lani. She tilted her head. "It must have been loose or something." The woman patted Lani's shoulder. "Are you all right, dear? That was quite the scare."

Lani's heart raced a mile a minute. She glanced around. Where was Oscar? "Did you see where my dog went?"

Both the old man and woman shook their heads. People had begun to move past her on the street, stepping around the pieces of the shattered air-conditioning unit. She stared through the forest of feet, not seeing the puppy as fear gripped her heart all over again. The poor thing had probably gotten frightened and run off.

A yelp came from inside the building. She pressed her face against the dusty window. She could just make out Oscar's face by a pile of scrap wood. The poor dog had been so afraid he'd run for shelter.

"Hang on, Oscar. I'm coming to get you."

She tried one of the double doors that were the main entrance to the building. Locked.

Oscar had gotten in somehow. She saw then a hole in the display window. Not big enough for her to slip through. She walked around to the side of the building and found a door that looked like it had been jimmied. Someone desperate for a place to sleep on a cold fall night had probably done that. Knowing that she might surprise someone, she pulled her gun.

She rushed in. She heard Oscar's whimper before she saw him in the dark corner. Broken display counters and pieces of mannequins still remained in the dust and debris.

A sense of relief flooded through her as she ran over to the puppy. She holstered her weapon and gathered him in her arms. "It's all right, buddy. That was scary for me too." The pup licked her face.

Thudding sounds came from the floor above her. Footsteps. Her heart beat a little faster. Maybe the air conditioner had had a little help by being pushed. Maybe the lock was jimmied by someone up to no good, not just looking for a place to sleep.

"Tell you what, buddy. You've had enough excitement for one day." She wrapped his leash around a door knob. She still hadn't been issued a new radio. Protocol would be to call for backup. That wasn't possible right now. She'd neglected to get another cell phone after hers was damaged by the water last night.

Chances were she was dealing with a vagrant, nothing more. He or she could have leaned against the air-conditioning unit…or the destruction might have been on purpose. Or just someone so high or drunk, they didn't know what they were doing.

Oscar yipped as if to offer encouragement. More footsteps sounded above her. She pulled her weapon and headed up the wide staircase in the center of the floor. The second floor was an open area with broken glass and display counters largely dismantled and probably used for firewood. Mattresses and dusty clothing scattered throughout the floor indicated the homeless had taken up residence at one time. Maybe they were still here. None of the big front display windows on this floor contained air conditioners.

She scanned the open floor area one quadrant at a time. There were places someone could hide, behind the piles of busted furniture and boxes and the display counters. She detected no movement. She held her own breath and listened, sensing that someone was watching her. Her mouth went dry. "NYPD. Please show yourself."

Turning quickly and aiming her weapon, she thought she saw someone in her peripheral vision. She let out a breath. Just a mannequin. She shook her head and dryly laughed.

There were smaller rooms on the south side of the building that might have been offices or storage spaces. Some had doors, some did not. With her heart drumming in her ears, she made her way toward the rooms.

Her own footsteps seemed to echo on the floorboards. The first room had no door, she peered inside seeing only empty shelving. She lifted her weapon and made her way to the second room. She held her gun in one hand while she opened the door with the other.

A hand went over her mouth and jerked her back. The attacker had come up from behind. "I got you." He pinched the nerves on her wrist. "Drop the gun."

Pain shot up her arm, but she held on to the gun. She angled her body side to side trying to escape his iron hold on her. In the struggle, she dropped her gun. She broke free, whirled around and slammed him hard in the stomach. The man, who was wearing a blue baseball cap, bent over. She scrambled to get her weapon.

The man recovered quickly and took off running just as she picked up her gun. Footsteps pounded behind her. Not another one. She whirled around aiming her weapon just in time to see Noah coming up the stairs.

On reflex, Noah pointed his gun at her. "Whoa."

Unable to form the question, she shook her head as if to ask what he was doing.

"I saw movement on the third-floor window where that thing fell out. I was just getting ready to walk around the corner to headquarters, but there was a construction accident that blocked the sidewalk, so it took me a minute to run back over here."

But he was here. That's what mattered.

She pointed. "He went toward the stairwell leading up."

They both raced across the floor. The culprit must have been trying to get out via the first floor when Lani had interrupted him on the second floor. Noah took the lead as they headed up the stairs.

The third floor consisted of a hallway and a series of rooms that were probably offices and storage. There was no obvious exit.

Lani pointed, signaling that they could work their way from either end toward the middle, clearing each room. She moved into the first room, cleared it and stepped back into the hallway just in time to see Noah disappear into a room on the opposite end of the hallway.

She stepped into the second room, which featured a large window that looked out on the street. A knocked-over file cabinet and pieces of a desk that must have been quite beautiful in its time cluttered the floor. This could have been the CEO's or store manager's office. There was no evidence a transient lived here, though she did see the hole that likely contained the air-conditioning unit that now lay in pieces on the street.

She shuddered. What was in the mind of someone who would push something out a window knowing there were people down below who could be hurt?

She heard the thunder of footsteps. Heart racing, weapon drawn, Lani stepped back out into the hallway just in time to see Noah sprinting toward the far end of the building.

Noah looked over his shoulder. "He's headed up to the roof."

Noah disappeared around a corner. Lani followed after him, praying they would catch their suspect.

Moments before, Noah had stepped out on a fire escape and spotted the suspect climbing out on a different fire escape and taking a ladder up toward the roof. He had raced back inside to see if there was an easier way to get to the roof. That's when he'd seen Lani and told her the suspect was headed up to the roof.

He hurried out to the landing where the suspect had

gone. The fire escape, which looked like it was hanging by maybe one bolt, was clearly not a safe route down. He peered up just in time to see the suspect's feet disappear over the top of the building.

Noah holstered his weapon and leaped up the uneven brick facade that the suspect had used as a sort of climbing wall. His muscles strained as he pulled himself up. He glanced down only for a moment to see the throngs of people and metal of cars glinting in the early morning sun. He found another foothold as his hands wrapped around the protruding brick above him.

Lani came out on the balcony. She groaned. "Are you kidding me."

Noah looked down at her. "Join the fun." He scaled the rest of the wall and pulled himself up to the flat roof. The suspect raced from one corner of the roof to another. He was trapped.

Noah pushed himself to his feet. He pulled his weapon just in time to see the man leap to the adjoining building. As chief, Noah was not out in the field enough to warrant having a radio. There was no time to make a call on his cell. He had to rely on Lani for backup. The suspect did not appear to be armed or he would have pulled a weapon by now.

He raced across the roof. There was about a five-foot chasm between the two buildings. Without hesitation, Noah pushed off. He stretched his right leg out in front, watching the edge of the building looming toward him. He landed with a thud. His knees buckled screaming with pain from the impact. The suspect had reached the edge of the second building. He hesitated, glanced back at Noah and then disappeared over the side. The guy must have found a safer fire escape.

Noah's heart pounded against his rib cage as his leg muscles strained. He sprinted toward where the suspect had gone. He peered down and saw only the top of his blue baseball cap. The guy had already made it to the top floor down the fire escape ladder. Noah swung down onto the ladder. He'd gone down only four rungs when Lani's voice reached him. She'd made up the distance between them pretty easily. "I'm going to look for a faster way down. See if we can cut him off."

He glanced up to see her head and shoulders as she looked down. Her bright expression and blue-eyed gaze met his. "Go find it."

She disappeared.

The suspect had only a short way to go down the ladder before he reached the street. Noah climbed faster narrowing the distance between them. When the suspect was halfway down the last part of the ladder, he jumped the remainder of the distance.

Lani emerged from the side of the building just as the man ran toward a crowded street market. She must have found an elevator in the building. Noah climbed two more rungs and then jumped, landing on his feet. He whirled around.

He could see Lani's blond head. She was in uniform but had lost her hat somewhere. The tight little bun on top of her head was easy enough to track in a crowd. He didn't see the suspect anywhere, but Lani ran like she still had sight of him.

He hurried past booths selling handbags and scarves. The aromatic scent of street vendor food swirled in the air, the mingling scent of salt, a heady sweetness and other spices. Noah kept his eyes on Lani. He didn't see the suspect anywhere. Still running, Lani merged with a throng of people. She towered above them. She stopped, glancing side to side.

He surveyed the area. Then he saw a blue baseball hat on the ground beside a food cart that sold gyros. The guy had ditched the hat knowing it would be an easy way to track him.

Lani turned back to face Noah, shaking her head before pushing deeper into the crowd. She wasn't one to give up easily even though he had a feeling the suspect had managed to give them the slip.

Taking slow steps, he ambled past the vendors, scanning the crowd one more time while he caught his breath. He didn't see the suspect anywhere. He retraced his steps, searching for the baseball hat thinking it might have DNA on it, but it had either been picked up or kicked out of view. He worked his way back to the edge of the street market, asking several of the vendors if they had seen the man in a blue baseball cap or seen a man take the cap off and throw it on the ground. All of them shook their heads.

When he glanced over his shoulder, Lani was headed toward him. As she drew closer, he knew that wrinkled forehead indicated her frustration.

She stood beside him and crossed her arms. "I guess that is that. I don't know what gets into people thinking it's okay to endanger public safety by pushing an air-conditioning unit out a window."

Concern niggled at the edges of Noah's brain. Lani had been attacked twice in forty-eight hours. "You don't think maybe that guy was aiming specifically for you?"

Her face went pale and she didn't answer right away. "He was probably just someone with mental illness issues or a drug problem. Don't you think? Besides, how would someone know that I would be walking by that building at that time?"

"You keep the same routine every day, don't you?"

"Well I...why would someone want to hurt me?"

"Do you think it might be the same man from last night?"

Her face blanched. "I didn't get a good look either time." She turned away from him. "I left Oscar back in that building by himself." She took off at a jog.

Lani clearly did not want to believe that the attacks were personal or connected. And he suspected she knew something she didn't want to share. Noah followed her back to the open side door of the building. They stepped from the brightness of day into the dim gloom of the abandoned building. Even the big display windows were so covered in dust not much light got in.

Oscar wagged his tail and yipped when he saw Lani. After untying him, she gathered the pup into her arms. "There's my little guy."

"Little guy?" Noah kneeled beside her, so he could pet Oscar's head and velvety ears. "Don't go all mushy on him. We're trying to turn him into a tough police dog." The dog licked Noah's face, melting his heart. So much for being tough.

"Oscar did all right. He did freak when that unit nearly fell on us, but he didn't seem too bent out of shape for having been left here." She let the dog kiss her face. "Next time you'll be a part of the action, won't you?"

Noah was concerned that Lani wasn't being realistic about the attacks. But grilling her wouldn't do any good. Right now, she was in denial. If he started slinging questions at her, she might become defensive.

He needed to get information out of her without making her feel pressured. "What do you say that after we get the crime scene people over here, I grab Scotty and we get Oscar used to working around people and staying focused?"

She put Oscar down on the floor and stood up. "That would be good for Oscar and for me. But do you have the time for that?"

The last thing he wanted to do anyway was sit in that office on this beautiful fall day. "I'll make the time." Maybe the attacks were random. He needed to make sure one of his officers was not in danger. That someone would not come after Lani a third time.

FOUR

Lani and Noah waited for the forensics team to show up at the abandoned building before heading back to headquarters. Lani loaded Oscar into the backseat of Noah's patrol car where Scotty already waited. Scotty remained at attention while Oscar jumped and nipped excitedly.

She laughed and shook her head. "Talk about the senior officer putting up with the rookie's misplaced enthusiasm." She ruffled the top of Oscar's head. Scotty let out a groan of protest. She reached across the seat past Oscar and stroked the Rottweiler's ear. "I love you too."

Scotty remained in position but licked his chops and leaned into her touch.

Lani climbed into the passenger seat. Noah already sat behind the wheel.

"The park is always a nice place to do training. Teach the dogs to deal with the distraction," he said.

She buckled herself in. "Yeah, sure." Her throat constricted. Noah was up to something. He wasn't in the habit of dropping his desk duties to hang out with her or any other rookie. Any of the other officers could have trained with her today. He'd wanted to know if she thought her attacker from the refuge and the one they'd chased in the abandoned building had been the same guy. The question made her chest feel tight.

While it was true, she hadn't got a good look at the attacker either time, there were similarities. Same height and build. But it was the assailant's unusual strength both times that made her wonder if they were dealing with the same man. Though she was a black belt and more agile than her attacker, he was an equal match for her due to his level of fitness. He'd spoken to her both times. She couldn't say for sure if the voice was the same. Why would anyone want to harm her though? That was what didn't make sense.

Noah pulled out onto the street and into traffic just as a call came over the radio.

"Missing child at the GallopNYC stables, Forest Hills."

"That's right up Scotty's alley." Noah picked up the radio. "This is unit twelve. Depending on traffic, I can be over there shortly with a K-9." Noah glanced over at Lani. "So much for a training exercise. This is the real thing."

Lani's heart beat a little faster. Though she was concerned about the missing child, the prospect of working a real case was exciting. She said a prayer of gratitude that she wouldn't have to deal with Noah's questions right away.

Maybe it was just the bliss of ignorance that she could be in denial a little longer. If the attacks were personal, would they let her continue in her K-9 training? She'd worked hard to get to this point. She didn't want to lose all that or even have it be delayed.

Noah wove through traffic with a high level of skill

by slipping into the pockets between moving cars and avoiding construction by taking side streets.

Noah checked his rearview mirror. "What's with this guy?"

Lani craned her neck at the line of cars behind them. "I don't see anything."

"That black sedan two cars back has been doggin' us since we left the station."

Her muscles tensed at the sight of the car.

Sensing her unease, Oscar leaped up and licked Lani's hand where she rested it on the back of the seat. She gave him a hand signal indicating he needed to sit. Oscar complied but shifted his weight from foot to foot as he sat back in the seat. He stretched his chin out indicating that he wanted affection from Lani.

Lani shook her head and waved her finger at the pup.

"He's a little unfocused to be good K-9 material," Noah said.

"He's still young. The initial testing showed he had a strong defense drive." She glanced one more time at the dark sedan. Encroaching fear made it hard to get a deep breath.

Noah hit his turn signal and slipped around a corner. After he'd driven several blocks, he checked the rearview mirror. She didn't need to look over her shoulder at the traffic behind them. Noah's expression, the tight lips and narrowed eyes, told her the sedan had turned as well.

The fenced dirt arena for the therapeutic horse stable came into view with the stables behind it. City apartment buildings and homes surrounded the little oasis for horses. She had volunteered here as a teenager. "I know the layout of this place."

A cluster of maybe ten people with two uniformed police officers stood on the edge of the arena. A rider—a young girl—with three adults, one on each side and one by the horse's head, trotted alongside the horse skirting the edge of the fence on the other side of the arena.

Noah pulled onto the grass beside the other patrol car where there was no fence. "I'm glad you know the layout. Let's go get the details from the uniforms." He got out, opened the back door and gave Scotty the command to hit the ground. Noah hooked the Rottweiler into his leash and headed toward the crowd. Lani glanced at the forlorn-looking Oscar. "You gotta stay in the car, buddy. Be good. We're both being tested." She shut the door just as the pup's tail thumped on the seat.

One of the officers noticed Noah and Lani. He broke away from the crowd. Lani recognized him from the academy. He'd graduated the same time she had.

She stepped forward. "Officer Langston."

Scotty sat at attention at Noah's feet.

Officer Langston was short and maybe twenty pounds overweight. His physical stature was deceiving. He'd played football in high school and was strong and quick on his feet. He smiled. "Officer Branson, good to see you." He tipped his hat toward Noah. "Chief Jameson. Just want you to know all the street patrol units have kept their ears to the ground for any news about your brother's killer."

A shadow seemed to fall across Noah's face at the mention of his brother's name. "Thank you, Officer." The change in mood was momentary. Lani wondered if she was the only one tuned into it. "Time is of the essence in finding this kid. What is the story here?"

"More tracking dogs and search-and-rescue dogs are

on the way." Officer Langston held up a child's red coat. "Brendan is five, he's autistic and deaf. He comes here for lessons. The usual thing. His mom was distracted for just a second. She turned back around and her son was gone. They searched the grounds for twenty minutes before calling us."

Lani didn't have to have Brendan's mom pointed out to her. It was clear the woman who gripped her purse to her chest with glazed eyes and an expression that looked like it was chiseled from stone was the distraught mom. They didn't need to make her more upset by peppering her with questions she had probably already answered. Officer Langston would give them all they needed to know.

Lani said a quick prayer for the mother and son.

"The mom says the son might think he's in trouble, so he'll hide," Officer Langston said.

And if the child was deaf, he wouldn't hear people calling for him.

Noah grabbed the coat and let Scotty sniff it. "Let's head up there and see what he can find."

"Two more dogs are on their way. I'm just glad you were able to get here so fast."

They made their way across the grounds toward the stables. Lani stared out into the streets that surrounded the little oasis of peace. Her throat tightened with fear. A five-year-old could wander out into the street pretty quickly.

"We've got a unit circling the block and officers on foot as well." Officer Langston explained before breaking away and heading back to where the cluster of concerned people huddled together.

Eager to work, Scotty lurched forward, causing the

long leash to go taut. They headed into the stables where
the boy had last been seen. A teenager stabbed hay with
a pitchfork and tossed it into a stall.

Scotty sniffed the ground. And hurried through the
building.

Lani lagged behind.

"You're here to find the kid?" said the teenager.

"Yes," she planted her feet. "Did you see anything?"

"No, I was in another building. All I know is that kid
loves animals. I can't help but think he was chasing after
a barn cat or became fascinated by a squirrel outside."

But where was he now? She didn't even want to think
about what could have happened to Brendan if he had
wandered off the grounds.

Noah exited the stables and headed toward another
building with Scotty sniffing the ground.

An idea flashed through Lani's brain. She called to
Noah that she would return quickly. She headed down
the hill toward the patrol car. She swung open the back
door and put a leash on Oscar. He ruffled his ears while
he licked her face. "Time for some on-the-job training.
Let's use your cuteness to draw out a little boy."

Oscar leaped down to the ground. They headed back
toward the stables. Her theory could be totally off base.
Something sinister could have happened to Brendan.
He could be miles from here by now. If he'd wandered
out into the street, someone in a car could have picked
him up.

She shuddered at the thought. Brendan was the age
of some of the kids in one of the martial arts classes
she taught.

Oh God, let there be a happy ending to all this.

She hurried across the arena just as another patrol

car with another search dog pulled up. She waved at the officer as he unloaded his dog. She caught up with Noah and Scotty inside a different barn that was filled with hay.

"Scotty loses the scent inside here." The barn appeared to be used mostly for storage of farm-type equipment, hay and other bags of feed.

"You think he's still on the grounds somewhere?" she asked.

"Yeah, but there are a thousand places where he could be. What if he's fallen and hurt himself." Noah's jaw tensed. "I hate when bad things happen to kids."

"Let's pray this isn't one of those cases."

Noah pointed at Oscar who tugged on his leash.

"The teenager feeding the horses said that Brendan loves animals. If he's hiding because he thinks he's in trouble, maybe a puppy will be enough to lure him out."

Scotty gave a soft alert to a smell by the door. They hurried outside and back around the grounds before returning to the storage barn. The barking and baying of the other search dog reached her ears. That dog wasn't headed in this direction. Either the other dog or Scotty had picked up on a false scent.

Scotty circled again, nose to the ground. Oscar nipped at the twirling dust in the sunbeams. Maybe the pup was too big of a goofball to be K-9 material. She suppressed a smile at the puppy's antics.

Lani studied the barn, which had a loft on one end where bales of hay and bags of feed were stored. Scotty kept coming back to this barn for a reason.

"I checked up there. I didn't see anything," Noah said.

She handed Noah Oscar's leash. "Hand him up to

me when I get up there." Even though the responding officer had said a search had been done, there were a thousand cubbyholes a kid could hide. And Brendan wouldn't be able to hear people calling for him.

"I'm going to search that loft." She climbed up the ladder. The platform was so stuffed with supplies she had to maneuver over the tops of the bags of feed to get to the corner. Lani sat down on a hay bale.

"Anything?" Noah's voice came from below along with Oscar's yipping and barking.

Lani sat very still as her eyes scanned every inch of the dark space. Gradually, her eyes adjusted to the light. Again, she studied the shadows until her gaze landed about a foot from the far corner of the loft where what looked like tarps were tossed in a pile. Beneath the tarps she was able to discern the tips of a child's fingers. Though she could not see a face or eyes she sensed that she was being watched.

Lani spoke. "Noah, can you get Oscar up here? And then run and get Brendan's mom. I found him."

"Sure."

Shuffling sounds came from down below while Lani remained very still. To move toward the child might terrify him even more. She listened to her own heartbeat drumming in her ears. Oscar's yipping grew louder. She turned to see Noah's head as he placed the puppy on a pile of feed bags.

Oscar made his way across the treacherous landscape while Noah remained at the top of the ladder. Oscar wagged his tail as he drew closer to Lani. She gathered the pup in her arms before setting him down, and Noah left to fetch the anxious mother. Judging from the position of the fingers, Brendan was lying on his belly peeking out from beneath the tarp.

Oscar sniffed around, stepped over a pile of hoes and rakes and headed toward the tarps.

The puppy sat down then looked over at Lani. Lani gave him the hand signal to lie down. Oscar complied.

The seconds ticked by.

Slowly, little fingers came out from underneath the tarp and touched Oscar's belly. Dragging his belly, Oscar moved closer toward the tarps and stuck his head in.

A giggle came out from beneath the tarp.

Tension left Lani's body like a hundred birds taking flight. Though Oscar had broken the ice, she doubted that Brendan would trust her, a stranger. And she didn't know sign language. Hopefully, Noah would be back with Brendan's mom soon.

Oscar came back out from beneath the tarp. The tarp lifted. She saw fear in the boy's expression and the round brown eyes. The boy remained very still as he pushed himself into a sitting position.

Lani hoped her hand signal communicated that she wasn't going to hurt him. She held a palm out toward him, indicating he could stay where he was.

Oscar licked Brendan's hand. The boy's fear seemed to melt as he gathered the pup in his arms and let it kiss his face.

Within minutes, Brendan's mother arrived to coax him out of the loft, hold him and reassure him that he was not in trouble.

While a crowd had gathered outside the storage barn, mother and son were left alone. Lani and Noah headed outside toward the patrol car with the two dogs in tow.

Scotty heeled beside Noah while Oscar galloped ahead, heeled for a moment and then got distracted by a bug.

Lani gave Noah a friendly punch in the shoulder. "See, even goofballs like Oscar can be helpful."

"I'm just glad this all ended on a positive note."

They arrived at the SUV. "I think the four of us make a pretty good team. Scotty knew that boy was in that barn. Oscar drew him out."

"And you knew enough to do a deeper search. And how to deal with the kid." Noah's hand brushed over her cheek. "Good job."

Her skin felt hot from his touch, though it was a gesture that he had done probably without thinking. Noah took a step back. The look of embarrassment on his face told her that he knew he'd stepped over a line.

She shook herself free of the heat of the moment.

Once her heart stopped fluttering from Noah's touch, she focused her thoughts on her work. A sense of satisfaction filled Lani as she loaded Oscar into the back of the patrol car. They did make a good team. She swung open the door on the passenger side and stared out at the busy street. Her mood took a nosedive as tension threaded anew through her body.

The dark sedan that had been following them earlier eased by on the street.

FIVE

As they drove back to headquarters, Noah knew Lani was upset. Not because her expression gave anything away, but because she was quiet. Lani had two speeds, fast and faster. If she was being silent, it meant something was wrong. He could understand her fear in seeing the sedan after the two attacks.

Noah turned on his signal and slipped into traffic. "We did good work back there." He'd already said as much at the stables but wanted to reiterate it. He checked the rearview mirror. No sign of the sedan.

She stared down at her fingers which were laced together. "Thank you." Her voice remained monotone.

He drove for several blocks struggling to figure out what to say to her that might alleviate her fear. Dealing with a woman's emotions had never been his strong suit. He'd grown up with brothers and his dating history was far from stellar. Most women told him he was too quiet and didn't give anything to the relationship or they didn't want to date a cop. Zach and Carter had both met wonderful women in the last few months. He was starting to feel like the odd man out.

He cut a look at Lani and shook his head. Why was he

thinking about dating at a time like this? He was Lani's direct supervisor, so that wouldn't even be an option.

Lani turned to stare out the window. "So what if this guy is stalking me." She shot him a quick glance. "I'm not quitting the force. I can handle this."

"No one says you have to quit, Lani." She might need to be put on desk duty though. He turned and headed toward Jackson Heights where headquarters was. He slowed down. "Look, it's past lunchtime. We can take a break, grab a bite at Griffin's. Maybe we can figure out who might be targeting you."

She massaged her temple. "Guess you already figured out it was the same guy from the refuge and the abandoned building."

"That's what you were thinking, right?"

"I didn't get a good look at the guy either time." Her voice faltered. "But the way he fought me...he didn't have any training, but he was really strong."

Without thinking, Noah reached over and patted Lani's shoulder. He pulled away after the second pat. What was it with this compulsion he had to offer her a comforting touch? When he'd brushed her cheek back at the horse stables, he'd felt a spark between them. A spark he would have to throw cold water on. He was her supervisor. Their relationship had to remain professional.

Lani stared out the windshield and let out a heavy sigh. "My stomach is growling. I could use a bite to eat."

Noah circled the block several times before a parking space opened up. With the dogs in tow they walked the few blocks to Griffin's. They moved past the counter with its round stools and the booths with worn vinyl seats. Noah always felt like he was stepping back in time when he entered Griffin's. It had been a cop hang-out for as long as Noah could remember. With more boutique-type stores and luxury high-rises taking over the neighborhood, Griffin's looked like a dinosaur.

Customers who weren't regulars at Griffin's craned their necks at the dogs. Some of the women made ahh sounds as Oscar pranced through the establishment with his head up. The people who ate at Griffin's all the time didn't even look up from their food.

Lani and Noah entered an area of the eatery set apart by a big sign that said The Dog House. The owners of Griffin's, Lou and Barbara, had always been supportive of law enforcement and especially the K-9 unit. Even more so since their daughter Violet had married Zach, Noah's younger brother and also a K-9 officer.

They hit the diner after the lunch rush, so only one other K-9 officer sat at a table in the corner. Gavin Sutherland recently had put in for a transfer out of the unit after getting engaged to Brianne Hayes, another officer, and word was that he was slated for a promo-tion to chief of a new K-9 unit that would be starting up in Brooklyn. Gavin offered them a wave as he sipped his coffee. His springer spaniel Tommy sat at his feet.

She glanced around the diner. Even for the off-hour between lunch and dinner, the number of customers seemed unusually low.

Lou Griffin set two menus down for Lani and Noah. "No Cobb salad today. Delivery messed up on the blue cheese order. The Philly cheesesteak is to die for."

Noah pushed the menu across the table. "Sounds good to me. And one of your chocolate shakes."

Lani flipped through the menu. "I'll have coffee, black, and the chicken sandwich."

"How's everything, Lou?" Noah hadn't had much of a chance to talk to Lou since Zach and Violet's wedding.

Lou shrugged his shoulders. He had dark circles under his eyes. "You know, the same old same old."

Lou and Barbara had been through a great deal in the last few months. A bomber had set up an explosive device in Griffin's to harm K-9 officers, but the owners had done the repairs and reopened. Last month, they'd closed temporarily due to health issues for both Lou and Barbara. Lou still favored the arm that had previously been in a sling.

Even if Griffin's did look out of place with all the new development going on, Noah could not imagine the neighborhood without it.

"You take care of yourself, Lou." Noah's heart went out to the man. "You look tired."

Lou waved his weariness away with his hand. "Ah, you Jameson boys. You are part of the family now." He clamped a hand on Noah's shoulder. "I suppose that means you can nag me about my health."

Noah nodded. "For sure."

Lou swiped the menus off the table. "Your order will be up in just a few." The older man sauntered away and disappeared behind the counter into the kitchen.

Lani took a sip of her water. "He seems really worn-out."

"Lotta pressure on him to sell this place," Noah said.

"Being a police officer in Queens wouldn't be the same without Griffin's," she said.

"I agree." Noah watched as Lani took another sip of water and then played with her silverware.

She sat back in her chair and stared at the ceiling for

a moment before looking directly at Noah with her soft blue eyes. "I guess we have to talk about the attacks."

Noah nodded. "I know this is hard to think about, Lani, but is there someone who might have a vendetta against you, maybe someone you arrested?"

Lani tugged at her collar as a patina of sweat formed on her forehead. Thinking that the attacks might be personal quadrupled the fear that plagued her. Oscar, sensitive to the drop in mood, licked her hand.

After stroking Oscar's soft head, she cleared her throat. "I haven't been on the force long enough or made that many arrests. Most of the arrests I made before getting into the K-9 unit haven't even gone to trial yet."

"So you just can't see anyone angry enough to attack and stalk you like that?" Noah ran his fingers through his brown hair. "And why is this happening now? Maybe one of the arrests you made is seeking revenge while he's out on bail."

She shook her head. "There were some drug arrests, but they were all small-timers, not smart guys. Following us to the refuge and lying in wait, knowing my schedule of walking the dogs, all of that takes some planning and intelligence."

"So not a criminal that you dealt with. Maybe some other part of your life, huh?" Noah threw up his hands. "The boyfriend of a rival model."

His tone was half-joking, but the comment cut deep. "I used to be a trained actress and dancer." She could not hide the hurt in her voice. "I was never a model."

Noah leaned toward her from the opposite side of the table where he sat. "I'm sorry. I was trying to be funny."

Regret clouded his expression. He reached across the table and squeezed her hand. "I was totally out of line."

She pulled her hand away, still hurting from the remark. "You know what my nickname is, don't you?"

"Here we go." Lou appeared holding two plates. He glanced at Lani who stared at the table and then at Noah whose gaze was downcast as well. "Looks like the food got here just in time."

They ate in silence for several minutes. Since the attack at the refuge, she had started to see a different side to Noah Jameson. He had seemed sensitive and caring. His hurtful comment blew all of that out of the water though. She salted her french fries and ate one in two bites.

"I know that some of the other officers think I can't cut it as a K-9 cop."

Noah put down his sandwich. "It's not that, Lani."

"It is that." She had started to think Noah had the same confidence in her abilities that she had. She knew she could be a great K-9 officer.

"Look, every time we step out onto the streets, our lives are on the line. The joking and the nicknames happen because of fear."

She shook her head. "I don't follow."

"Other cops just want to know you have the skills in a tight situation. Your résumé isn't exactly the normal path a cop takes." He took a sip of water.

She nodded. Her irritation over his comment softened. "So the other officers wonder if I would have their backs in a tight situation or if I would just break into song and dance." She smiled.

Noah laughed, almost spitting his water out.

Lani laughed too. All the tension she'd felt melted away.

"What you did today in finding that kid, your tenacity in chasing the suspect at the refuge. And I know you shot a suspect in your own house when you were off duty. You are cop material, Lani."

Lani looked into Noah's green eyes, feeling a connection to him. She'd waited to hear those words for months.

Noah said, "I'm going to let it be known that the nickname is not funny." He smiled. "I am the chief, you know. I do have some say over what kind of atmosphere is set for the unit."

"Thank you." She took a bite of her sandwich. "Maybe we can speed up the process of assigning me a dog."

"Yeah, I just don't think it's going to be Oscar."

She laughed and petted the pup's head. "How is your milkshake?"

He sipped some through his straw. "Wonderful as usual." He tilted the tall glass toward her. "It's thick enough to eat with a spoon. Help yourself."

She scooped out a spoonful. She allowed the creamy sweetness of the ice cream to melt in her mouth.

It was nice to be with Noah in an informal setting. Both of them seemed to relax as they finished their meal and talked about inconsequential things.

As they left with their dogs, Lani caught a glimpse of Lou and Barbara in the kitchen. Both of them looked tired. They'd been through so much in the last few months. She'd heard that a real estate developer had offered them a great deal of money for Griffin's. But it wasn't Griffin's he wanted, it was the lot. If Lou sold, Griffin's would no doubt be torn down. And something

more in line with the gentrification of the neighborhood would take its place. That possibility made her
heart heavy.

Noah kept pace beside her as they skirted around
the clusters of people on the sidewalk. Both of them
fell silent when they walked past the abandoned building where the air conditioner had been pushed out a
window.

Her gaze traveled upward as a shiver traveled down
her spine. Oscar sat back on his haunches. Was the
puppy remembering the trauma that had taken place?
Lani tugged on Oscar's leash.

Noah edged a little closer to her, so their shoulders
were nearly touching while Scotty remained on the
other side of him, alert and standing. Unlike Oscar,
Scotty was unfazed by the people swarming around
them.

Noah must have picked up on her fear. He was pretty
adept at reading her even though they hadn't spent that
much time working together closely.

"So what do you got on the agenda for the rest of
your shift?"

With Oscar still squirming at her feet, she turned to
face him. "It's a split shift. I'm going home to get some
rest and then I will be riding with Brianne and Stella
for the night patrol."

Noah's expression changed. He wasn't a man who
showed much emotion. Maybe she was reading too
much into the crease between his eyebrows and light
dimming from his green eyes, but she thought she detected concern for her in his features.

"You be safe out there," he said. "I've got to get back
to my desk. I'm sure things have been piling up." He

glanced around. "Why don't you walk the rest of the way with me back to headquarters?"

Her car was actually several blocks from headquarters, but she needed to see that Oscar got back into his kennel. Even if she didn't have a dog to return, she would have said yes. There was something nice about being with Noah Jameson.

As they walked with the late-day sun warming her skin, she felt light-headed. Her heart fluttered a little when she cut a glance toward Noah, who offered her a smile. She shut down the feelings of attraction as quickly as they had risen to the surface. He was her supervisor and she was probably reading all kinds of things into his vague expressions that were her projection.

As police officers, they'd had a good shift. Any day where a kid was returned safely to his mom was a good day. That's all they were to each other. Two cops who wanted to keep the people of New York safe.

Lani said goodbye to Noah, watching him head toward his office, before returning Oscar to the kennel. He'd go home to his foster family in the evening and be returned for testing the next day. Though Noah didn't seem to have much confidence about his abilities.

Traffic back home was a bear this time of day and she found the fatigue settling into her bones as she waited several cars back at a light. When she got home, there was a note from Reed saying he was having dinner with Abigail and then taking in a movie. Jessie was with Dominic so they could bond more. Dominic was the teenage boy who Abigail and Reed intended to adopt once they were married.

The note said that he probably wouldn't be home

until after ten. Reed was spending more and more time
with his fiancée, which was how it should be. Yet she
felt the emptiness of the house with both Reed and Jessie gone. Just weeks ago, the house had seemed so full.
Abigail and Dominic had stayed here for a bit because
both had been in some danger. In addition to all the
people, a female pup of Stella's named Midnight had
stayed with them. Now Abigail was fostering the puppy
at her apartment. Lani stood at the kitchen sink staring
out the window at the empty yard in a quiet house. The
upstairs tenant wasn't even walking around.

Still full from the late lunch, she had a snack of al-
monds and blueberries and set her alarm. As was part
of her routine, she made sure the doors were locked and
latched before she lay down for a nap. Her last thought
before she drifted off was of Noah's quiet demeanor
and soft smile. If today had proven anything, it was that
her initial impression of him, that he was the cold one
amongst the Jameson brothers, had been wrong. Noah
was one of those men who warmed up to people slowly.
He was slow to trust and open up, and maybe that was
a good thing. Until their lunch together, she hadn't realized that he had a sense of humor.

She let out a heavy sigh. Why was she even thinking
about Noah and his green eyes? What she wanted more
than anything right now was to prove that she could be
a great K-9 cop. She felt like at least Noah had more
faith in her now. He had seen what she was capable of.
She remembered what Noah had said about the other
members of the unit having confidence that she would
have their backs in a tough situation. She needed to
show them that was true.

She awoke several hours later to what sounded like

someone moving around in the kitchen but trying to remain quiet. Reed. Maybe he had decided not to go to the movie with Abigail.

She rolled over and closed her eyes. It was only a little after eight. She could get a few more hours of much-needed sleep.

The noises in the kitchen stopped and she heard footsteps approach her door and then pause outside.

The ticking of the clock seemed to grow louder as she waited for Reed to walk past.

Lani sat up. Fully alert and staring at the door. Reed would not be lingering outside her door. She reached for her gun which she'd put on her nightstand like she did every night. The last thing she wanted to do was shoot her brother by accident, but she didn't want to take any chances either.

Heart pounding, she opened her mouth to say her brother's name. Her throat constricted. No words came out.

The footsteps resumed and headed back toward the living room. Lani took a deep breath before rising to her feet. Still gripping the gun but holding it by her side, she stepped toward her bedroom door and turned the doorknob slowly.

She moved down the hallway. She took a deep breath and found her voice again. "Reed, is that you?"

Silence.

Her heartbeat drummed in her ears as she crept lightly down the hallway. She raised her gun, prepared to fire. She stepped into the dark kitchen seeing only shadows. She flicked on the light switch. Everything seemed to be in its place.

But her heart wouldn't stop pounding. Had the attacks made her so hypervigilant that she was imagining her stalker was in the house?

As she entered the living room, she kept her gun aimed. She checked behind the couch and anywhere else someone might hide. Nothing.

And still, there was a faint unfamiliar smell in the air. Not cologne or Reed's soapy clean smell, more like sweat.

Lani dropped her arm that held the gun, so it hung by her side. She shook her head. She cleared the rest of the house, checked that the doors were still locked and was headed through the living room to try to get some more sleep when her eyes fell on the photo wall.

Her breath caught. The photo of her posing in a dance costume was gone.

A wave of fear crashed over her as her knees went weak. She turned a half circle in the living room, took a deep breath and moved through the house a second time.

How could someone have gotten in with all the doors locked? She examined the bathroom window closer to find the latch had been forced, which would have taken substantial strength. She stood on the toilet to peer at the ground below where a stack of bricks that must have come from the remodel two houses down had been piled.

Lani sat down on the closed toilet, feeling as if all the wind had been knocked out of her. She placed her gun on the sink counter. Of course she'd have to file a report, but that could wait. If Noah found out, he might put her on desk duty and she'd miss out on the valuable in-field experience and a chance to show the other officers what she could do. She could call Reed and let him know.

She wrapped her arms around herself and waited for her heartbeat to slow down.

Why me? Why am I being targeted?

Ever since Jordan Jameson's murder, the entire K-9 department had been on edge. Not only because they wanted to catch whomever had killed Jordan, but because anytime an officer died in such a premeditated way, the whole department wondered if they were dealing with someone who might go after other cops.

She was the obvious target. The least experienced. The rookie. The taking of the photo did suggest something more personal. Yet her stalker had had the chance to do her harm in her own home and hadn't. Almost as though he enjoyed the psychological torture. She shivered, clenching her teeth against the terror that raged through her.

Her thoughts were interrupted by a tapping on her front door that caused a new wave of terror to wash over her. Why was the person knocking so lightly?

Grabbing her gun, she stepped into the living room but remained paralyzed, not sure what to do given what had just happened. Certainly, the stalker wouldn't come to her door.

SIX

Noah hoped his knock on Lani's door wasn't too loud. If she was still sleeping, she wouldn't hear it at all. He wiped the sweat from his brow. He couldn't say exactly why he'd changed up his jogging route so it ended at Lani's house. Just a feeling he'd had, concern for one of his fellow officers' safety. Scotty sat beside Noah, panting from their run.

He leaned close to the door, tapping it with his knuckles. "Lani, it's me. Noah."

What was he going to say to her? That he was in the neighborhood and thought he'd stop by. How cliché. Before he'd gotten off shift, he'd overheard Reed talking about his date plans with Abigail. That meant Lani was alone for most of the night until she went back on duty.

While he'd been on his jog, he couldn't let go of the worry that she might be in danger. He just needed to make sure.

He heard the peephole slide open and then shut. The dead bolt and the lock released and Lani swung the door open.

He knew immediately from the spasm of a smile she offered him that something was up. Her face was pale, and her gaze seemed to dart everywhere and she was holding her gun in her hand.

"Noah." Relief came into her voice when she said his name.

His heart fluttered.

"We were jogging, and I thought I'd check on you." He pointed at the gun.

"Guess I'm a little freaked because of the attacks." She stepped to one side so he could enter the living room. "I can protect myself." She placed the gun on a table.

Noah and Scotty came inside. He took Scotty off of his leash so he could explore with his nose. He studied Lani for a moment. She massaged the back of her neck, not making eye contact.

He stepped toward her. "Everything okay? I didn't wake you, did I?"

She shook her head. "No, I was up."

Why did he feel like she was keeping something from him? He angled his body so he could peer into the kitchen.

But there was no one in the kitchen.

"I'm alone here," she said.

"You seem uncomfortable, I thought maybe you had a boyfriend or someone over for a bite to eat before you went to work."

She shook her head. "I'm not seeing anyone. I haven't dated for a long time." Her tone took on an edge to it.

Was that pain he detected beneath her words?

All the same, he was glad to see her. The tightness through his chest deflated like a balloon to know that she was safe. Why was he relieved that she wasn't seeing anyone? Her personal life was just that, personal.

He was here at her doorstep over concern for a fellow officer, wasn't he?

Satisfied, Scotty stopped sniffing around and came to sit at Noah's feet.

"Tell me again why you stopped by." A look of confusion crossed her features. The blue in her eyes intensified and her mouth drew into a flat line.

"I, um...we." He patted Scotty's head. They were in this awkward moment together. "Well, it was sort of on my jogging route."

Scotty adjusted his stance and made a grunting noise.

Lani laughed. "Scotty does not agree with you."

Noah could feel the heat rising up in his cheeks. He held his palms out to her. "Okay, I was out jogging and I knew that Reed would not be home tonight and given what happened to you in the last couple of days, I thought I should check on you."

Her expression brightened. "You were worried about me."

"Yes, I don't want anything bad to happen to one of my officers."

All the light seemed to leave Lani's face. "Oh."

Scotty grumbled again.

Mentally, Noah kicked himself. Why were they doing this strange dance? Why couldn't they just admit their attraction to each other and acknowledge that nothing could come of it?

"Anyway, I suppose I should go. Scotty and I need to get tucked in for the evening." He turned then pivoted back to look at her. "Everything is okay here, right?"

Her lips parted slightly as though she were going to say something, and then she turned away from him and started to straighten the pictures on the wall and sweep her hand over a shelf that held more photos and ballerina figurines.

The soft lighting in the living room made her look even more attractive. He wasn't used to seeing her with her long blond hair flowing freely. Her cheeks held a rosy glow. She was beautiful inside and out. He stepped toward her as though there were some sort of magnetic pull between them.

"Lani, is everything okay? I know you have been through a lot in the last couple of days."

She planted her feet and turned to face him. "Everything is good. I'm sure if we put our heads together we can figure out who this guy is, and I can get on with my training. That is what I want."

Noah nodded.

She picked up one of the figurines and turned it side to side. "I keep wondering. With what happened to Jordan. What if it isn't personal? What if someone is targeting the K-9 unit?"

Noah let out a heavy breath. That thought had occurred to him too. "It's hard to figure out motive at this point. Let's just focus on catching the guy."

"I suppose you're right." She stepped back toward the door. "I need to get ready for my shift."

"Yes, well, Scotty and I are going to enjoy an evening of popcorn and a John Wayne movie," he said.

"I love John Wayne."

"Maybe sometime you'll have to come over and watch one with us. Scotty and I are doing movie night alone a lot more since Carter got engaged and Zach got married."

"I know the feeling. Since Reed met Abigail, we

spend a lot less time together, which is how it ought to be but still, it leaves a hole."

He met her gaze. Looking into her eyes sent a spark of electricity through him. "Well, that's something we have in common." He stepped toward the door.

She leaned toward him. "I'm glad you stopped by to check on me."

"Everything is okay, right?"

"Yes."

He studied her for a moment. It was as if a veil had fallen across her eyes when she answered him. "Hope your shift goes good."

"Yeah, I better get moving." She ruffled Scotty's head. "I'll take you guys up on that movie offer some time."

She closed the door. Noah stood for a moment staring at the door before clicking Scotty back into his leash and jogging toward his house.

Though it was clear that she was all right, he couldn't help but feel that Lani was hiding something from him.

Before she headed out for her night shift with Brianne, Lani gave her brother a call to let him know what happened. She hated interrupting his time with Abigail. Reed as always sounded glad to hear from her.

She let him know about the break-in and the stolen photo.

"I'll grab Jessie from Dominic's place and come right home," he said.

"No, Reed, it's okay. I'm headed out for a shift in a few minutes. I just need for you to make sure the place is secure when you get home. I'll be fine once Jessie is able to sound a warning bark and you're here."

"Sis, this is serious, why didn't you call the department and file a report?"

Lani squeezed the phone and closed her eyes. "I will file a report. I didn't want to miss out on my shift tonight. It's a valuable learning experience to shadow a more experienced female officer. I'm just afraid when Noah finds out, he's going to put me on desk duty."

"Maybe, Lani, but it would be for your own safety."

Tears warmed Lani's eyes. "I don't like setbacks. It's been hard enough to deal with the delay in matching me with a K-9 partner. I know I sort of took the long way around, but I want to be a part of this K-9 unit more than I've ever wanted anything else. This whole thing feels like an obstacle to that."

"Look, Lani, I know you. Whatever you set your mind to, you accomplish."

A tear trickled down her cheek. Until now she hadn't realized how much the attacks were affecting her. "Thanks, Reed. If you could just make sure the home is secure when you get back from your date. Say hello to Abigail and Dom for me and tell her I'm sorry for interrupting your time together."

"I'll do better than that, sis. I'll wait up for you."

"Thanks, but just having you home will be enough. And can you look at the latch on the bathroom window. I think it will need to be repaired." She had come to depend on the sense of safety she felt when he was around. "I'll be fine while I'm on this shift. There's no safer place to be than on patrol with a K-9 and her handler, right?"

"Right."

"I'll catch up with you later. Take care, Reed." After he said goodbye, she ended the call. A set of headlights went by on the street outside moving slowly. A moment of panic gripped her until she saw under the streetlamp that it was a patrol car. Brianne Hayes was looking for a parking space.

Already in uniform, Lani grabbed her utility belt and hurried to the bathroom to place her gun in the holster. Before leaving the house, she took in a deep breath and stepped outside making sure the door was locked behind her.

Brianne eased past the house. She must have seen Lani because she double-parked. Lani ran to the passenger side of the car, and Stella whimpered from the backseat when Lani got in.

Brianne offered Lani a bright smile. Her straight auburn hair was pulled back into a ponytail. Brianne had always been kind to Lani. "Ready for some night patrol?"

Lani nodded. She reached back and ruffled Stella's head. "How's my girl? I was just working with one of your pups."

"Ah yes, Oscar. What a cutie. Gavin said he saw you at Griffin's with him, Noah and Scotty." Brianne lifted her chin. "He said you looked very cozy." Gavin and Brianne had recently become engaged.

"Cozy?"

"Like you'd known each other forever."

Lani felt the heat rise up in her cheeks. "We were just trying to figure out the motive for the attacks on me. I'm sure you've heard."

"Yes. I heard." Brianne turned onto a street that led to a freeway exit. "Everyone gets uncomfortable when a fellow officer is attacked."

Tension invaded the patrol car. "We still don't know if this is personal or because I'm a cop."

Brianne let out a nervous laugh. "Maybe we should talk about happier things."

"I agree. How is Stella doing with her training?"

"Stella's coming along," Brianne said. After signaling, she pulled back out into traffic. "Unless we get another call, we're headed over to some abandoned warehouses. We've had several calls of suspected drug activity. We'll see how Stella does with her drug detecting training."

Lani felt a surge of excitement at the prospect of working with Brianne and Stella to make the city safer. Even with everything that had happened, she loved police work. "It's nighttime. There might actually be some activity there."

"Maybe. If we find or see anything drug related, the detective division might set up some stakeouts to see who the players are and what the level of activity is." Brianne picked up speed once they were on the freeway.

She took another exit and wove through an industrial part of Queens. They passed parking lots that had only a single car parked in them, probably belonging to a security guard. Some of the multistory buildings had a light or two still on.

They came to a chain-link fence, the gate of which hung open. Brianne eased the vehicle inside. The tires crunched on gravel. "A few days ago the trustee for the property got a call that the chain that held the gate had been cut. Someone also reported seeing a car go in here."

Most of the buildings inside the fence were one or two stories and metal, with the exception of a square brick one that must have held the administrative offices.

Lani's heart beat a little faster as she stared out into the darkness. "What's the story on this place?"

"I think the report said it used to be a textile factory.

They imported lots of fabric too, so some of these buildings were for storage and warehouse sales. Hasn't been used for at least ten years."

Stella let out a single excited bark.

"You're ready to work, aren't you?" Lani pushed open her door. "Me too."

Once they were out of the car, both women pulled their flashlights from their utility belts. Brianne attached the leash to Stella's collar. "Let's head toward that first building and see what we find."

Lani shot her flashlight in an arc taking in her surroundings. There was no sign that anyone had been here. No tire tracks or empty soda bottles, not even any trash. Stella darted toward the first long narrow building. Maybe the witness had been mistaken about a car coming in here.

As the two women raced toward the first building, Lani asked, "Is there another way out besides that front gate?"

"The report didn't say." Brianne was breathless as she ran to keep up with Stella. They searched the area all around the three buildings. Though it was hard to see in the dark, it looked like there might be another entry point on the other side of the property. In the distance, cars and trucks whooshed by on the highway, a million tiny bug-like lights. Beyond that, the tall buildings were dark shadows with only a dot of light here and there. Lani pictured a lawyer hunched over his desk in that lighted room or maybe it was a late-night cleaning crew.

In searching the property, Lani had gotten separated from Brianne and Stella. She could hear Brianne giving words of praise and commands to Stella who yipped from time to time. There were no excited barks indicating Stella had found something.

Lani thought she saw movement on the far end of the fence. Heart racing, she ran toward it. The flashlight illuminated her path. She stopped twenty yards from the fence and aimed the light all along the fence. Was that the glint of metal? A parked car maybe? She stepped closer to the fence.

A noise by the square metal building, something banging against something else, caused her to pivot. Fear invaded her awareness. She had a moment of wondering if her stalker had followed her here. She shone the light just in time to see a dog racing for the cover of a pile of wood pallets. The animal turned and looked in the flashlight beam, its eyes glowing red. Her breath caught. It wasn't a dog, it was a coyote. The animal disappeared into the darkness.

Footsteps behind her caused her to swing around. Brianne's light bobbed up and down as she came toward Lani.

"I'm not finding anything. Let's see if we can gain entry to any of the buildings. We have permission."

Lani hadn't gotten a chance to search the remainder of the fence to see if there was a car there.

They hurried back toward the long narrow building. Lani shone her flashlight on the door, which held an open padlock. She checked the bottom of the padlock where the key went. Scratches around the keyhole indicated someone had picked the lock.

Lani pushed open the door and it screeched on its hinges.

Stella let out a nervous whine. With only a little

moonlight shining through the small high windows, the building was dark.

Both of them stood on the threshold for a moment before stepping across. The eerie quiet made Lani's heart pound.

Once inside the building, Brianne let Stella off her leash so she could sniff around. She shone her light wherever the dog ran. "Even if she alerts to something, we'll probably have to get a more experienced K-9 out here to confirm."

Lani shone her flashlight into the dark corners of the building. There were huge metal vats that must have been used for dying fabric. A conveyor belt took up most of the center of the room nearly touching each of the far walls.

There was no sign of occupants after the factory closed. This place was too out of the way to be appealing to the homeless or even teenagers looking for a cool hangout.

Though she continued to sniff, Stella hadn't alerted to anything. Lani strode to the end of the building taking the rickety stairs up to peer inside the giant metal bowl. It looked like there was some sort of object in the vat. She stood on tiptoe and raised her flashlight to get a closer look.

On the other side of the building, Stella barked incessantly. Brianne screamed and dropped her flashlight. Lani's heart squeezed tight with fear as she ran across the factory.

SEVEN

Lani dashed toward the ruckus Stella was making. She stumbled over a pile of metal, catching herself before she hit the floor.

Stella had gone ballistic with her barking. Racing back and forth and then alerting to something high up.

Brianne crawled across the floor to recover her flashlight, which was still on but had rolled beneath a table.

Lani pulled her weapon.

Stella's barking was relentless, which only fueled Lani's excitement mixed with some fear.

Brianne rose to her feet. "No need for the gun." She spoke above Stella's barking. "Stella, back, quiet."

Stella obeyed, sitting but shifting her weight and whining.

Brianne shone the light up toward where Stella had focused. Tiny black eyes stared back at them, a cornered raccoon, probably as scared as they were. The raccoon skittered away across the high shelving and through a hole in the roof.

Brianne shivered and shook. "Critters give me the heebie-jeebies." She reached out and touched Lani's forearm. "Don't tell anyone I screamed and dropped my flashlight. I can just imagine the nicknames that will come from that."

"I know all about nicknames."

They both laughed.

"I think Stella freaked just because she's never encountered a raccoon," said Brianne.

A screeching noise from the other end of the dark building alerted them. They both darted toward the sound, which had come from the far side of the vat Lani had peered into. Stella ran alongside them.

Lani circled around the metal vat, which had a hinged door on it. She swung the door open. The package she'd seen inside earlier was gone. Noise like footsteps above them caused Brianne to shine her light just in time to see a man moving along the high shelving and out the same hole the raccoon had gone.

They raced toward the door. Brianne and Stella went in one direction toward where the hole in the roof was while Lani went in the other. They'd be able to get the suspect regardless of what direction he ran. Lani radioed for back up.

The far side of the long building was dark. Lani shone her light toward the ground where rubble and debris created a sort of obstacle course. She ran as fast as she dared. When she came to the end of the building, she shone her light all around the property. She caught an occasional bark and yip from Stella some distance away but nothing else.

Her chest felt like it was in a vise making it hard to get a deep breath. She stood paralyzed for a moment. The silence was oppressive. Again, she wondered if her stalker had followed her out here. She shook off the fear and continued to search.

It didn't matter if the stalker was here or not. He was inside her head now. She would always be wondering if he was close, watching and waiting.

The inflection of Stella's bark changed, becoming more frantic. Lani moved toward the sound, shining her light in an arc across her path. She saw shadows, a man running with Stella at his heels. But Brianne was nowhere in sight.

The man yelled in pain as Stella jumped and wrapped her mouth around his upper arm. Lani raced toward where Stella had taken down the suspect. She pulled her weapon. What had happened to Brianne?

"Get this dog off of me," the suspect yelled.

Lani gave the command for Stella to let go. Stella backed off but stood alert, emitting a small growl.

The suspect held his hands close to his upper body probably to protect himself. "Look, I'll do whatever you want just don't let that dog attack me again."

Lani dared not take her gun off the suspect to look around for Brianne. She heard the sirens in the distance. Backup was on the way.

Footsteps pounded behind her and she caught a glimpse in her peripheral vision of Brianne running and holding her arm.

"Took a tumble back there. Glad you and Stella were here to back me up."

"He must have dropped that package somewhere," said Lani.

"I know about where. We'll find it. My guess is it's not a box of chocolates. It's probably drugs, and he was the pickup man."

As the sirens drew near, Lani gripped her gun, letting a realization sink in. Tonight had turned out good.

They'd gotten their suspect. But she knew now she wouldn't be able to give a hundred percent to her police work as long as the stalker was out there. If she was distracted and fearful wondering when the man would make an appearance again, she was a risk to herself and others. Like Noah had said, the other officers needed to know she had their backs.

She'd have to tell Noah what had happened and agree to go on desk duty. As the sirens for the other police cars drew closer, she vowed to put all her energy into finding the stalker and seeing that he was put behind bars, so she could have her life and future as a K-9 officer back.

As he scrolled through the pages on his computer screen, Noah found himself distracted by Lani's presence as she sat in the desk normally occupied by his newlywed assistant, Sophie, who had gone on her honeymoon with K-9 officer Luke Hathaway.

Noah hit the print button.

He was glad that Lani had come clean with him about the home entry. And that it was probably her stalker. He didn't like there being secrets between them. That the stalker had entered her home was disturbing.

The temp they'd hired to take Sophie's place had not worked out, so it seemed a logical solution to put Lani in the desk where he could keep an eye on her.

After grabbing the pages he'd printed, he stepped toward his open doors with some paper in hand watching Lani as she tossed some crumpled paper toward the wastebasket. She pushed herself back from the desk in her roller chair several times.

Noah smiled.

She had a harder time sitting still than he did.

Patricia Knowles, the receptionist for the K-9 unit, came toward Lani, holding a bouquet of flowers. Lani stood up. Her hand went to her heart and he saw her mouth the words *For me?*

An unfamiliar surge of emotion invaded Noah's awareness. So Lani was getting flowers. Why did that bother him?

He stepped closer to her desk putting the papers on it. "Flowers, huh?"

Smiling, Lani pulled the envelope from its holder. "I have no idea who they're from." She opened the envelope and read the note. She dropped it as though it was on fire.

"Lani?"

She shook her head and stepped away from the desk. Putting trembling fingers up to her face.

He rushed toward her, touching her elbow lightly before turning and picking up the note. He clenched his teeth when he read the note.

I love you and I am watching you always.

Lani slumped down in her chair and put her face in her hands. She looked defeated and afraid.

Uncertain of how to handle Lani falling apart, Noah went into fix-it mode. "Let's find out who dropped these off."

He examined the flowers and the container they came in to make sure there was no camera or bomb or anything that might do harm. After dismantling the arrangement, it appeared they were just dealing with flowers and a note designed to keep Lani afraid.

Lani crossed her arms over her chest and looked off

to the side. Her voice was weak, a million miles away. "He wouldn't be so dumb as to drop them off himself. I'm sure he had a delivery service give them to Patricia."

He hated seeing her so distressed. It made him feel helpless. "We can do a little detective work." The envelope had the name of the florist stamped on it. "After work, we can go to the shop and find out if the clerk remembers who placed the order." She continued to stare into space.

He studied the note. It was typed, probably by the florist. The purchase might even have been called in or ordered online. He was grasping at straws, trying to find a way to get Lani to not shut down.

She shook her head, gazing as though she wasn't really seeing.

Promising solid police work wasn't helping. He kneeled and pulled the chair toward him, forcing her to make eye contact. "Lani?"

She looked down at him. The veil seemed to fall away from her eyes. "Noah, no matter what? He can get to me. I'm sitting at a desk in a building with armed police officers."

Noah glanced at the note again. "Well, he's obviously a liar. He's not watching you right now. There's no way he could get past security. You have to be issued a visitor's badge to get access to this part of the station." He tried to keep his tone light. "Right?"

She lifted her chin slightly. And released a single-syllable laugh. "Is that the bright side of all this?"

"Look, I'll stay close to you. When I can't, we'll make sure another officer is around to check on you. It doesn't have to be official. I'm sure any of these guys would give up some off-duty time to provide protection for you."

"I hate that I need the protection. I should be the one doing the protecting. I want to do my job."

He was grateful that Lani had perked back up. That was the Lani he knew and respected. "Thank you for not giving up."

"The only way I can do my job is if we put this guy away."

Figuring out the guy's psychological profile would help with catching him. "This note sounds almost… romantic…in a twisted way."

"I know. Maybe this isn't because I'm a cop," she said. "I started to wonder if maybe someone had a beef against the department and I was the easiest one to target 'cause I'm the newest recruit."

"Yes, the note implies something different."

She rose to her feet and took in a breath. "Guess I better do my job." She pushed some forms toward him. "You need to sign off on these. It's just order forms for supplies for the dogs and then I'll take it over to the training center to make sure it's all good."

Noah picked up a pen and signed the forms. "Couldn't you just email it to the supply officer?"

"I like seeing the dogs. It calms me down."

"I'll go with you. Maybe we can brainstorm who might be sending you this kind of note."

"What do you mean?" She gathered up the papers and headed toward the door.

Noah walked beside her as they headed down the hallway toward the stairs that led to the training center. "So if it's not someone you arrested or someone who has a beef against cops, maybe it's someone who liked or likes you in a romantic way, maybe an ex-boyfriend."

She walked a little faster holding the forms close to her chest. "Maybe."

"I'm not meaning to pry, but did you date anyone in the past who struck you as unstable?"

She walked even faster, he had to double his pace to keep up.

"Selfish, yes. Unstable, no," she said. "Give me some credit."

Her tone was almost defensive.

They entered the training center where Tony Knight was working with his chocolate Lab, Rusty, running him through an obstacle course on the AstroTurf flooring. A look of concern crossed Tony's face when he saw Lani.

"Okay, so maybe someone who might want revenge," Noah said.

"It's really hard for me to talk about my dating life. I haven't been out in over a year by choice." She met his gaze, her eyes rimmed with tears. "Honestly, if anyone had cause for revenge, it would be me for the way I was treated, not the other way around." She walked away toward a door where the supply person probably was.

Noah shook his head. He could kick himself. He'd only wanted to get to the bottom of who was after her so she would feel better, safer. Instead he'd struck a nerve and made her sad. He remembered something his mother had said to him that men, especially Jameson men, always wanted to fix everything and sometimes women didn't want things fixed. They just wanted someone to listen.

Maybe he should just try to be her friend. She'd talk

if and when she wanted to. As much as he wanted the stalker behind bars, pressuring Lani would only backfire. She had enough to deal with.

Lani returned, running toward Noah, her face etched with worry. Tony Knight was right behind her with an equally concerned look on his face.

"What's up?" A sense of dread settled into his bones.

"It's Oscar. Someone has snatched him."

Tony came up behind Lani. "It was my turn to walk him and work with him out on the street. I made him sit and stay while I went into a store. When I came out, he was gone."

EIGHT

Lani clicked through the screens on her computer, then hit the print button for the forms she needed to leave on Noah's desk before she quit for the day. It had been two days since Oscar had gone missing, presumably stolen, and her heart was heavy from the loss. It was so easy to get attached to the dogs. Another of Stella's puppies, Midnight, had been at the Branson home quite a bit since Abigail was fostering her during her training.

She'd checked the website of local shelters as well as ones where missing pets were posted. The other officers had put up lost posters around the city. Still, no one had phoned in about the puppy.

Oscar's disappearance brought back the emotional impact of the loss of another dog. Snapper, Jordan Jameson's K-9, had been missing since the former's chief's murder. The German shepherd had been spotted around the city, and then Dominic had admitted that someone had given him a dog that matched Snapper's description, but the shepherd had run off. Snapper was alive somewhere. And one of Stella's other puppies, Cocoa, had been taken briefly as well but was now home safe. She didn't see any that resembled Oscar or Snapper.

Lani closed the website containing postings of found pets. She had to believe that Oscar was alive as well. Someone probably took him for a pet because he was so cute. Or thought he was valuable because he wore a vest that said he was a K-9 in training.

She left the forms on Noah's desk. His meeting with other precinct chiefs must be running late. The preparatory meetings for security at the Columbus Day Parade required coordination between all the boroughs. Plans were being made for some of the K-9s and their handlers to march in the parade as well. She had no idea what her role would be for the big event. Maybe she wouldn't be permitted to help at all. The confinement of sitting behind a desk was taking a toll on her.

What she liked about police work was how active it was. But now, she couldn't jog or ride her bike in the park alone anymore. Though Noah and Reed both offered to go with her, she missed the alone time when she could clear her head and pray.

The one bright spot about feeling like a prisoner because of her stalker was that she and Noah had spent more time together. She found herself looking forward to being around him. She was glad he hadn't asked her about her dating history again. The whole thing was so painful. Men tended to see her blond hair and blue eyes and nothing more. She was a whole person, and she wanted to be loved for who she was inside and out. It was better to be alone than with someone whose attraction to her was only skin-deep.

She placed the forms on Noah's desk and gave Scotty's head a pat from where he lay on his dog bed. She kneeled so the dog could lick her face.

"What a good boy," she said. "And your boss isn't a bad guy either."

After texting Noah that she was leaving for the day, she grabbed her purse and headed out of the building toward the parking garage. The text was a courtesy. She was a trained officer, she didn't need an escort to the parking garage. The police lot was for NYPD vehicles only. Her personal car was in the parking garage not far from headquarters. Her feet seemed to echo on the concrete as she walked toward the elevator that would take her to the third story where her car was parked.

She watched the numbers light up. The door slid open and she stepped out onto the concrete. As she walked toward her car, she heard the sound of a car pulling out and racing down the ramp to the exit.

Some people were just anxious to get home on a Friday night. She had no plans other than to stay in, make some popcorn and find a movie to watch. The thought that maybe she could take Noah up on watching a John Wayne movie together put a smile on her face.

When she arrived at her car, there was a folded piece of paper on the windshield. She assumed it was some sort of solicitation or announcement of an event. She reached for the paper.

Her breath caught in her throat.

None of the other cars had the paper on them.

A sense of dread fell on her like a lead blanket as she opened the folded paper careful to only touch the edges in case there were fingerprints on it. The note was neatly typed in a squarish font.

I took Oscar because I know you love him. Next time it might be your brother or that other cop you've been hanging around so much. I have that kind of power. Say you love me, and I'll give you back the dog.

Feeling as though she'd been punched in the stomach, Lani turned and leaned against her car for support. She opened her purse, feeling for the gun she always kept there.

She listened to cars on the floor above her pulling out and rolling down the ramp. The sounds from the street, traffic and people, reached her ears.

She took a deep breath to calm herself. With her hand still on the gun in her purse, she pushed off the car and surveyed all around her. The note could have been placed here anytime while she was at work. Maybe her stalker was long gone and maybe he was keeping his promise and watching her always.

She could hear but not see cars pulling out and gaining speed. Footsteps echoed somewhere on the other side of this floor of the parking garage. But she could not see anyone.

Her heart squeezed tight, and the blood whooshed in her ears.

She tilted her head. Maybe the parking garage camera had picked up the stalker when he'd placed the note.

Her phone buzzed. A text. The number was Noah's. She clicked on it. Somehow even a text from him made it easier to breathe.

Where are you?

In the parking garage.

Another text from a different number came in. Out of habit, she clicked on it.

I am watching you always.

Lani's gaze darted all around the garage. She felt light-headed as she took in several shallow breaths. Though he could be texting from anywhere, it couldn't be coincidental that she'd read the note and then the text had come through. He knew what time she got off work and when she would be at her car.

Her phone dinged again.

She didn't have time to answer it, didn't want to answer it. She pulled the gun from her purse and placed it on the hood of the car. She fumbled in her purse for the keys. Her fingers trembled.

She had been as cool as a cucumber dealing with potentially violent people when she'd been on regular patrol and when an intruder had entered their home. But this was different, it was personal.

She pulled the keys out and pressed the unlock button.

Footsteps moving at a rapid pace sounded behind her. She whirled around not seeing anyone.

"Lani?"

The voice was Noah's. Relief spread through her and she was able to take a deep breath. "I'm over here."

More pounding footsteps. Noah with Scotty beside him came into view. Though she remained standing, her knees felt like cooked noodles. She hadn't realized how afraid she was until she saw Noah.

"Hey, I was worried about you when you didn't answer my second text." His voice filled with compassion as he stepped toward her. He must have seen something in her expression despite her best effort to hide the fear that had been like a wave pulling her under.

She cleared her throat. "He found me again." She wanted to crumple the note and tear it to pieces, but knew she needed to keep it pristine if they were to get any DNA off it at all. She lifted it toward Noah.

Noah took the note and read it. His jaw grew tight and hard indicating that he was upset, maybe even angry.

"Then…he…sent a text." Her voice faltered. She couldn't be the hard as nails police officer, not under these circumstances. "I'm sorry. I didn't mean to fall apart."

"Anyone would." He gazed at her with a welcoming softness in his green eyes. "You've been stronger than anyone I've ever worked with Lani."

It felt as though a weight had been lifted off her and she fell into his arms. He wrapped his arms around her. "It's okay," he said. "It's going to be okay."

She relished the warmth and comfort of his arms. How safe it felt to be held by him. Her cheek brushed over his collar and she took in the musky aroma of his cologne. She tilted her head to look into his eyes. "Thank you for understanding." A tear rolled down her cheek. "I know it's not very professional…to lose it like this."

He reached up and swiped the tear away with his finger. His touch was as gentle as a feather brushing over her skin. "I think we are more than just colleagues, don't you?"

Her heart fluttered. "Meaning?"

"I consider you a friend, Lani. I hope you see me in the same way."

What had she thought he would say? And what was this pounding heart and ooey-gooey melting feeling inside her belly all about. "Yes, friends." Even if he was attracted to her, Noah was too much of a man of integrity to ever cross a line. There could never be anything but a friendship between them.

She took a step back trying to escape the magnetic pull being close to him created. It wasn't just the attraction that was a problem. The truth was she felt safer when he was around. She wasn't sure that kind of dependence on him was a good thing.

She studied him for a moment. For his meetings today, he'd dressed in a light blue button-down shirt, khakis and a camel hair coat. She had thought he looked quite handsome when he left the office earlier in the day. She had teased him and now she reminded him of her comment. "You still look like you are ready for the opera."

"Yeah, opera's never been my thing."

Noah was one of those guys who could dress like he was ready for a business meeting, and he could pull off the jeans and T-shirt look just as easily.

Scotty whined and adjusted his stance.

"Well, I suppose I better get home." She turned back toward her car. "I'm glad you showed up when you did."

"Got a big Friday night planned?"

"Not really, just going to go home and find a funny movie."

"I suppose Reed will be out with Abigail."

"Once he gets off duty. That's usually what he does."

"Listen, I have a favor to ask of you since you don't

have anything planned." He touched the collar of his coat. "At the meetings today, it became obvious to me that there is an expectation that as chief I ought to be rubbing elbows with—" he made quotations marks with his hands "—the important people of New York."

"You have to attend some kind of event?"

"Yes, at the Bayside Historical Society. A lot of big-wigs will be there." Noah stared at the ground, shoved his hands in his pockets and kicked at nothing. "I've never been good at that sort of thing…schmoozing. You're so articulate and outgoing. It would be great if you came with me."

This was a side of Noah she had never seen, such vulnerability. "I'd like that. It won't take me long to shower and change."

"Great. How about I follow you partway out to your house, before I turn to get to mine. And then if you could text me that you got there safe, I'll come by in an hour."

"That sounds good." She gave Scotty's head a rub, which made his tail wag.

He waved the note the stalker had left on her car. "Of course, we'll take this in to Forensics."

Her mood shifted. "I'm worried about Oscar."

He exhaled through his teeth. "Clearly we are dealing with someone who is not only unstable but not very logical. He says you get Oscar back when you declare your love for him." He shrugged. "How would you even do that? Are you supposed to text him that?"

She shivered. "Maybe he'll communicate further. If he comes out into the open, we'll be able to get him, right?"

He squeezed her arm. "I don't like the idea of you being bait."

"It might be the only way," she said. "I don't get my life back until this guy is behind bars." Her voice sounded strong, but her insides still felt like gelatin.

"Let's not think about it right now." He pointed across the parking garage at where his car must be parked. "Why don't you pull out. Let me and Scotty get back over here and then we'll follow you. I'll drop this note off at Forensics in the morning."

She nodded, got into her own car and exited the space. Soft instrumental music played on her sound system while she watched her rearview mirror until she saw the headlights of Noah's car. She could just make out the outline of Scotty's square head in the passenger seat. She rolled down the ramp and out onto the street.

It got dark around dinnertime this time of year. The city was already lit up. She pulled out into traffic. Every time she checked her mirror Noah was right behind her. She felt a sense of loss when he turned off to go to his house.

Lani circled the block before a space opened up a few blocks from her house. She hurried home, unlocked the door and the dead bolt, and stepped inside the quiet house. After making sure the door was locked behind her, she switched on lights. She was glad Reed had met Abigail, but getting used to being alone was a challenge. Reed and Abigail were always inviting her to their activities, but they were in love and surely wanted time alone. Plus they were becoming instant parents because of Dominic. They had enough on their plate.

She was grateful for Noah's invitation. She liked the idea of being friends with him.

She headed toward her room to pull something from her closet to wear. She'd had to attend galas and fund-raisers when she was doing theater and dance, so her wardrobe of evening wear was extensive.

Have gown, will travel.

She smiled and shook her head at her own joke.

She was glad to have somewhere to wear the gowns. It was nice to have something to do on a Friday night with someone she liked being with. She suspected one of the reasons Noah had invited her was because he didn't want her to be alone in her house.

As she showered and then dressed, a thought weighed heavy on her mind. The stalker had figured out that she was attached to Oscar. Next time, would he go after a person that she cared about, like Reed or maybe even Noah? The note had said as much.

NINE

Noah found a parking space on the street opposite Lani and Reed's house. He walked across the street feeling a sense of anticipation. When he had thought about having to go to one of these functions alone, all he'd felt was dread. He knocked on the door. His shoulder holster dug into his chest when he lifted his arm.

Even when he was off duty he carried a gun, especially now that Lani's safety was under threat. He heard the lock open and the dead bolt click back. Lani opened the door.

Noah nearly fell backward at the sight of her. His knees felt mushy. She wore a long light blue dress that brought out the blue in her eyes. Her hair was pulled up on top of her head in a loose bun with soft curls framing her face. Her skin glowed like she'd put some sort of glitter on it.

He shook his head and managed only a single word. "Wow."

She smiled faintly. "Believe it or not, I've had a lot of practice with this dressing up and schmoozing."

Still not able to catch his breath, he held an elbow out for her. "Shall we?"

She stepped across the threshold and then turned to secure the door, pulling a key out of the tiny beaded purse she held.

As they crossed the street to his car, Noah's stomach felt like it was filled with melting wax. His throat had gone dry. He hurried around to the passenger side of his car and opened the door for Lani. He caught the faint scent of her floral perfume as she got inside.

She lifted her chin and locked him in her gaze, which made him feel like he might fall over.

"This should be fun," she said.

He nodded, unable to form any coherent words. On the walk back around to the driver's side of the car, he gave himself a combination pep talk and kick in the pants.

Come on, Noah, pull it together. This isn't junior high.

Noah got behind the wheel and offered Lani a grin that he hoped didn't look too dorky. He pulled out onto the street. He drove through the neighborhood and then got on the Van Wyck Expressway.

Lani went into her usual hundred mile an hour talk. He was grateful he didn't need to do much talking due to the fact that he'd lost the ability to form words.

She finished her story and then fell silent for a moment. "It's nice to be able to get out and do something social."

"I'm sorry having this stalker at large limits your ability to do things. Maybe if we can figure out his motive, it would be easier to catch him. You never finished answering my question. Do you think an old boyfriend might be stalking you?"

"It would have to be from a long time ago. I gave up on dating."

"Really?" Why would someone like Lani not want to date?

She didn't answer right away. "I don't know how to explain it exactly. It's like all men see is who I am on the outside, and they don't want to get to know me in a deeper way. Even Christian guys."

Hadn't he just been guilty of kind of the same thing? Making assumptions about her because of her background and if he was honest because she was pretty. Images flashed before him of Lani showing so much compassion to the boy with autism at the horse stables. "As your friend, I'm telling you they missed out on getting to know a really great person."

"Thank you."

"Lani, I've underestimated you in a hundred ways. If I ever made you feel like one of those boyfriends, only seeing who you were on the surface, I'm so sorry."

Noah veered onto the Cross Island Parkway. It was about a half-hour drive from Rego Park to the historical society.

He took the exit and drove up Totten Avenue. The parking lot was about half-full when he pulled into it. The building that housed the historical society was also known as the Bayside Castle. With its striking red and white brick structure and turrets it was aptly named. The castle had once been part of a working fort where soldiers stayed.

Noah got out of his car and hurried around to open the door for Lani. She stepped down and straightened the skirt of her dress. Made of layers of sheer fabric, the dress made a sort of whispering rustling sound as they walked toward the double doors of the castle. Light spilled out from within and he could hear the sound of people visiting and laughing.

They entered a long wide hallway with wooden floors. People were gathered in clusters of three and four, sipping drinks and eating from small paper plates.

"So I guess we just wander, right?" Noah said as a note of sadness filled his voice. "My brother Jordy was always better at this sort of thing than me."

She leaned close to him, wrapping her arm around his. "Don't worry, the time passes quickly."

The castle contained rooms for dining, rooms that had rotating displays of art, and some permanent collections of both art and artifacts. He knew from having come here as a kid with his brothers that they had exercise classes and activities for children. They walked past a room where a quartet played classical music.

They wandered into a room that had been turned into a sort of labyrinth because of the way the temporary walls that displayed artwork had been set up. A man with a tray wandered by and Noah grabbed two glasses of water from him.

Lani took her glass.

A man walked toward them with his hand outstretched. "Noah, so glad you could make it." Noah knew he'd met the man previously, but he couldn't quite place him.

"And who is your lovely date?" The man turned toward Lani.

"I'm Lani Branson, I'm with the K-9 unit Noah oversees, Mr. Liscomb."

"Delighted," said Mr. Liscomb.

The three of them exchanged small talk about the

event and food with Lani carrying the conversation before Mr. Liscomb faded into the crowd.

Noah leaned close to her and whispered in her ear. "How did you know his name?"

"I checked the city council website before we came here while I was getting ready. Mr. Liscomb oversees the committee that decides how the law enforcement money gets distributed."

"Yeah, I guess I did meet him. Just don't remember where." He tugged at his collar, which felt tight. His neck was sweaty. He wanted to get out of the tux and into a pair of sweats and a T-shirt. "Honestly, this is not my thing. I'm glad you're here."

She tilted her head, blue eyes shining. "I'm glad I'm here with you."

Noah's heart fluttered. Somehow, he wished he could stay in this moment with Lani gazing at him with such warmth and affection. "We make a good team."

"Yes, we work well together." She laughed. Then her expression darkened, and she took a sip of water, turning to look at a painting.

He felt the drop in mood. He touched her shoulder, wanting to ask her what she was thinking about.

She turned to face him, that sad look on her face. Her lips slightly parted.

"Hey," he said. "Everything okay?"

Was she thinking about the stalker or was it something else?

"I'm fine." The shadow across her face told a different story. For the next half hour, they talked with other city officials and people of influence. With each interaction, Noah was glad Lani was there to make the conversations go more smoothly. She had a wonderful understanding of art, theater and all the stuff he knew very little about.

Instruments being played in an adjoining room rose to a crescendo. "Why don't we go listen to some music?"

"Sure," he said. Again, Lani had that faraway look on her face. Something was on her mind.

He knew better than to press her about what was on her mind. She'd share when she was ready.

They stepped back out into the hallway.

She touched his arm. "I think I'll go find the restroom and then meet you in there." She pointed toward the room where the musicians were playing.

"Sounds good." Noah wandered across the hall just as the violin trilled with intensity. He glanced over his shoulder in time to see the effervescent skirt of Lani's gown disappear around a corner.

Noah gulped his water and set the glass on a side table where a waiter swooped it up. It felt awkward standing and listening. A woman came up and introduced herself as the mayor's wife. Noah chatted with her for a moment, wishing Lani with her easy laugh and knowledge of the arts was standing beside him.

The musicians completed their piece and were well into another when Noah began to wonder what was keeping Lani. Even if there was a line to use the bathroom, she should have been back by now.

A knot of tension formed at the back of Noah's neck. He stepped toward the threshold to go in search of her.

A short man and a woman with a tiny dog in her purse approached him. "Chief Jameson, how good to see you."

"Councilman." He couldn't remember the guy's name. "Good to see you too."

Noah could feel himself growing restless and worried as the councilman and his wife kept him trapped in conversation about nothing. The knot of tension in his neck got even tighter.

He waited for a polite moment to excuse himself. Worried, he hurried down the hallway in search of Lani.

Lani watched the warm water from the bathroom faucet spill over her hands. The line for the downstairs bathroom had been long, so she'd slipped upstairs to find one. All the planned activity was on the first floor. Only a few people wandered the hall upstairs.

She stared at herself in the mirror. Why had Noah's remark about them working together so well hit her so hard? The truth was she was starting to have feelings for Noah, deep feelings.

His remark had caused her to envision having a life together. Such as being a support for him at these gala events that he didn't much like. Somehow when they were together, it ended up being an adventure. She saw them jogging together in the park with Scotty or going to church together. Gripping the countertop, she wiped the pictures from her mind.

She'd closed her heart off to the possibility that she'd ever meet someone special, but now she felt her heart opening to Noah. And he was not available. He was her boss.

Lani grabbed a paper towel and dried her hands. She stepped out into the silent hallway. Laughter, music and party chatter floated up from the first floor. She wasn't ready yet to go back downstairs. She walked down the hallway and stepped toward the window that looked out on the parking lot and the city beyond all lit up like a Christmas tree.

Footsteps pounded behind her. When she turned to see who it was, no one was there.

Lani's pulse drummed in her ears. Her chest squeezed tight with fear. "Hello." The footsteps had been distinct. Could it be that someone was working late and had slipped into one of the upstairs offices? That was the explanation that made the most sense. This was what the stalker had done to her mind. Even when he wasn't close, he had power, control even, over her.

The safety of the crowd was just downstairs. All she had to do was walk to the opposite side of the hallway where the stairs were. Easy-peasy, right? Lani took in a deep breath. She strode past locked office doors. The men's bathroom was at the end of the hall by the window. So whoever was up here wasn't in there. Still, she had heard someone.

She stood before a room not too far from the staircase. The door was ajar, but it was dark inside. She pushed the door open farther and reached a hand inside the room, searching for a light switch. Once the light was on, she eased the door all the way open.

It was a sort of storage room. Framed photographs and paintings were stacked against the walls. There was a suit of armor and a garment rack where costumes were hung. File cabinets and shelves with labeled bins cluttered the chaotic room.

She cleared her throat. "Hello." She reminded herself that the safety of the crowd was just down the stairs. There was a part of her that wanted to overcome her fear. She'd always thought of herself as a strong woman. What kind of officer would she be if she couldn't face the thing that she was most afraid of? But more than anything she just wanted to catch this guy and put him behind bars.

While her heart pounded in her chest, she surveyed the room inch by inch. Sweat trickled down the back of her neck.

A single bumping sound reached her ears before a mass barreled into her and pushed her to the ground. She lay there staring at the ceiling, the wind knocked out of her. The man had on a face mask so she couldn't see his face. He pinned her to the floor by holding her shoulders down.

"Now I've got you."

Terror raged through her.

"Lani?"

The voice was Noah's.

The attacker lifted his head, alarmed by the voice. He bolted up and ran out of the room.

She managed to sit up by the time Noah was by her side. She gripped his arm. "It was him."

He helped her to her feet. "Did he hurt you?"

She shook her head. "I'm okay. I think he knew he would be caught if he hung around." Her head cleared. "I heard his footsteps. There must be a back stairway." She hurried down the hall to the window she had stared out earlier.

She spotted a dark figure moving toward a cluster of trees not far from the parking lot.

Noah dashed toward the stairway. "Maybe we can catch him before he gets to his car."

She hurried after him, grateful she'd worn flats not heels. With Noah in the lead, they sprinted across the grounds toward the parking lot.

"Stay with me." Noah pulled his gun out.

"Wouldn't it be better if we split up to look for him?"

"Maybe but I don't want to risk you being hurt or kidnapped."

Somewhere in the lot, a car door slammed. The sound seemed to reverberate.

Lani stepped toward Noah. They wove through the lot up one row and down another. All the cars remained dark. A couple holding hands came out of the building and headed toward the parking lot.

Noah put his gun behind his back, probably so the man and woman wouldn't be alarmed. They waited while the couple got into their car, pulled out of their space and headed toward the street.

Just as the couple turned onto the road, tires screeched behind them. Lani whirled around to the blare of two headlights charging at her. Noah pulled his gun as the car zoomed toward them.

TEN

Noah wrapped his free arm around Lani and pulled her out of the path of the car. They fell hard on the concrete, his gun dropping to the ground. He rolled off of her, angling his body just in time to see the car turning around to take another shot at them.

He grabbed Lani's arm and pulled her to her feet, then guided her in between cars as the stalker's car barreled toward them. Tires screeched. They came to an open area that led to the next row of cars.

"Let's make a run for my car. You go first. I'll be right behind you."

She sprinted out, the skirt of her dress flying behind her. He was at her heels, aware of the sound of the stalker's car zooming through the lot toward them.

The headlights were only feet away when Noah swung open the driver's side door and jumped in. The car whizzed by scraping the side of his vehicle, knocking off the side view mirror so it hung by a single wire. Another second of delay and it would have torn his door off.

Lani sat in the passenger seat. Her dress was torn. Her hair had shaken loose. She had a dark smear across her cheek. She'd lost her purse in the struggle. She was beautiful still.

He pulled his phone from his pocket.

He tossed the phone toward her. "You want to call for backup?" He shifted into Reverse and pulled out of the space. "Let's give this guy a run for his money."

The stalker had turned his car and was circling back around to come up behind them again.

Lani phoned into the station, gave their location and the situation.

Noah zoomed up the row. He took a turn so tightly the car seemed to be on two wheels. He could see the stalker's car moving through the lot as he pressed on the gas. The plan was to come up behind the guy. Without a gun, he had no recourse but to try to disable the car with his own.

He sped up another row as the stalker turned and headed toward the exit. So the guy knew that he didn't stand a chance if he stayed in the lot.

They raced out onto the road. Noah was concerned about leaving his gun behind but there was no time to go look for it. Once they were on the expressway, traffic was heavy enough that keeping up with the car was a challenge. Though he hadn't lost sight of the stalker's car, several cars had slipped in between them.

"If we can just get close enough. I can at least get a read on his license plate," Lani said. "Everything happened so fast. I didn't notice the plate when we were in the parking lot."

Noah stared straight ahead. "Let's see what we can do." He waited for an opening in the next lane and slipped into it, pulling ahead so they were two car lengths behind the stalker.

Lani shifted in the seat, lifting her head and leaning toward the side window, trying to get a view of the license plate at the odd angle.

The stalker took the next exit without signaling first. There was no time for Noah to switch lanes before they passed the exit. Noah clenched his jaw. They'd lost him.

Lani sat back in her seat. "I couldn't see to get the numbers." Picking up his phone she quietly called off their backup.

They drove on in silence for a while longer. The look on her face nearly tore his heart out. "We'll get him, Lani. Call it in and Forensics can go over where he was hiding."

"There's probably a million fingerprints in that room." The tightness in her voice revealed her frustration. "His car was generic looking. Maybe there were some cameras that will show the plate number."

"Maybe," she said, not sounding very hopeful.

A tension-filled silence invaded the car. He'd do anything to make her feel better, lift her spirits. He felt a connection to her that he didn't quite understand. His mood mirrored hers.

"Sorry about your dress," he said. "You looked really beautiful tonight."

"Thank you." She smoothed over her torn skirt. "We have to catch him, Noah. I want my life back. That's all there is to it."

"I should not have let my guard down back at the castle," he said.

She let out a heavy breath and massaged her forehead. "It's not your fault. I should be able to go to the bathroom alone. Right?" She laughed and shook her head. "Okay, it is a little bit funny."

He was glad she hadn't lost her sense of humor.

Though he still felt the weight of her frustration and fear, the levity was a nice reprieve. "So when does Reed get home?" He liked the idea of spending another hour or two with her even if they just drove around and grabbed a cup of tea somewhere.

"I'm not sure. I can text him." She pressed her palm to her forehead. "My purse. I dropped it. Probably when he knocked me over."

"We can go back and get it." He searched the exit signs calculating how to get turned around. It took a good twenty minutes to get turned around and headed back to the castle. "The celebration is probably just breaking up," he said. Really it didn't matter to him what they did. He just liked being with her.

When they arrived, the lot was less full, but the lights were still on inside.

Noah and Lani searched the lot until they found his gun twenty minutes later.

By the time they got to the building, the cleanup crew was busy pulling tablecloths off of tables and hauling out bags of trash. The musicians packed up their instruments. Only a few people lingered, caught up in some intense conversation.

"The upstairs is closed to the public now." A woman with a clipboard caught them at the base of the stairs. She had small intense eyes and tight lips. "Can I help you?"

"I dropped my purse upstairs."

The expression on the woman's face indicated that she required more information.

"I used the upstairs bathroom earlier this evening. I left my purse up there. I think in that storage room,"

Lani said. She turned toward Noah, touching the lapel of his coat. "We won't be but a minute."

"That room is locked. I'll go up with you," said the woman.

Lani stepped in behind her and Noah followed.

Once they were in the upstairs hallway, the woman opened the door for them, flipped on the light and stood back. "This room should have remained locked during the festivities. There are some valuable artifacts in here. It was an oversight on the staff's part."

The woman with the clipboard seemed like an uptight, by-the-rules kind of person.

Lani stepped across the threshold and stared at the floor. "It's not here."

"I can tell you right now, no purses were turned in to the lost and found," said the woman with the clipboard.

Noah stepped in as well and surveyed the area. "It looked like an antique. Maybe it just got picked up." He stepped toward a rack of costumes, searching.

"Please don't touch anything," said the woman.

There were several beaded dresses that looked like they were from the 1920s. Lani's purse was hung up with one of the dresses on the hanger. She reached for the hanger. "I can prove this is mine." She said to the woman.

Lani's deference to the woman indicated that she was having a similar reaction to her. Noah felt like he was back in second grade again with Mrs. Pendleton, the meanest teacher he'd ever known.

Lani pulled the purse strap off the hanger and put the dress back on the rack. "My phone and my license are in here." She clipped the purse open so the woman could see.

"All right, then," said the woman. "I've got a great deal to do before we shut off the lights."

YOU pick your books —
WE pay for everything.
You get up to FOUR New Books and TWO Mystery Gifts...absolutely FREE

Dear Reader,

I am writing to announce the launch of a huge **FREE BOOK GIVEAWAY**... and to let you know that YOU are entitled to choose up to FOUR fantastic books that WE pay for.

Try **Love Inspired® Romance Larger-Print** books featuring Christian characters facing modern-day challenges.

Try **Love Inspired® Suspense Larger-Print** novels featuring Christian characters facing challenges to their faith... and lives.

Or TRY BOTH!

In return, we ask just one favor: Would you please participate in our brief Reader Survey? We'd love to hear from you.

This FREE BOOK GIVEAWAY means that we pay for *everything!* We'll even cover the shipping, and no purchase is necessary, now or later. So please return your survey today. You'll get **Two Free Books** and **Two Mystery Gifts** from each series to try, altogether worth over **$20!**

Sincerely,

Pam Powers

Pam Powers
for Reader Service

Complete the survey below and return it today to receive up to 4 FREE BOOKS and FREE GIFTS guaranteed!

▼ DETACH AND MAIL CARD TODAY! ▼

FREE BOOKS GIVEAWAY
Reader Survey

1

Do you prefer books which reflect Christian values?

◯ YES ◯ NO

2

Do you share your favorite books with friends?

◯ YES ◯ NO

3

Do you often choose to read instead of watching TV?

◯ YES ◯ NO

YES! Please send me my Free Rewards, consisting of **2 Free Books from each series I select** and **Free Mystery Gifts**. I understand that I am under no obligation to buy anything, as explained on the back of this card.

❏ **Love Inspired® Romance Larger-Print** (122/322 IDL GNUN)
❏ **Love Inspired® Suspense Larger-Print** (107/307 IDL GNUN)
❏ **Try Both** (122/322 & 107/307 IDL GNUY)

FIRST NAME	LAST NAME

ADDRESS

APT.#	CITY

STATE/PROV.	ZIP/POSTAL CODE

© 2019 HARLEQUIN ENTERPRISES LIMITED
® and ™ are trademarks owned and used by the trademark owner and/or its licensee. Printed in the U.S.A.

READER SERVICE—Here's how it works:

Accepting your 2 free books and 2 free gifts (gifts valued at approximately $10.00 retail) places you under no obligation to buy anything. You may keep the books and gifts and return the shipping statement marked "cancel." If you do not cancel, approximately one month later we'll send you 6 more books from each series you have chosen, and bill you at our low, subscribers-only discount price. Love Inspired® Romance Larger-Print books and Love Inspired® Suspense Larger-Print books consist of 6 books each month and cost just $5.99 each in the U.S. or $6.24 each in Canada. That is a savings of at least 17% off the cover price. It's quite a bargain! Shipping and handling is just 50¢ per book in the U.S. and $1.25 per book in Canada*. You may return any shipment at our expense and cancel at any time — or you may continue to receive monthly shipments at our low, subscribers-only discount price plus shipping and handling. *Terms and prices subject to change without notice. Prices do not include sales taxes which will be charged (if applicable) based on your state or country of residence. Canadian residents will be charged applicable taxes. Offer not valid in Quebec. Books received may not be as shown. All orders subject to approval. Credit or debit balances in a customer's account(s) may be offset by any other outstanding balance owed by or to the customer. Please allow 3 to 4 weeks for delivery. Offer available while quantities last.

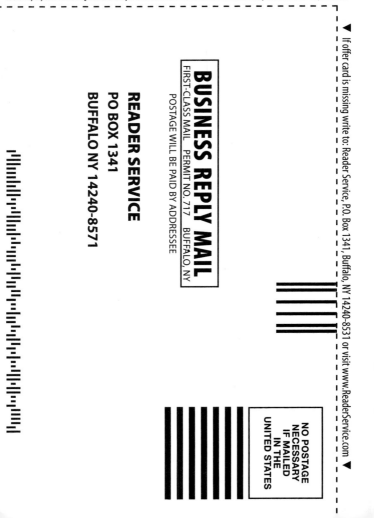

▲ If offer card is missing write to: Reader Service, P.O. Box 1341, Buffalo, NY 14240-8531 or visit www.ReaderService.com ▲

BUSINESS REPLY MAIL
FIRST-CLASS MAIL PERMIT NO. 717 BUFFALO, NY

POSTAGE WILL BE PAID BY ADDRESSEE

READER SERVICE
PO BOX 1341
BUFFALO NY 14240-8571

NO POSTAGE
NECESSARY
IF MAILED
IN THE
UNITED STATES

Noah held out a hand for Lani. He was anxious to get away from the uptight woman with the clipboard.

Lani stepped toward him but then froze in place. The rosiness faded from her cheeks as she stared straight ahead.

"What are we waiting for, then?" said the woman.

Lani shook her head and rushed toward Noah who wrapped his arms around her. "What is it?"

Lani pointed at a bunch of framed photographs stacked against the wall. Noah followed the line of her gaze.

The photo of Lani as a dancer lay on the floor. The attacker must have dropped it. She stepped closer to peer at it. A red *X* had been drawn over her face.

Lani gripped her stomach, feeling suddenly nauseous. Noah wrapped an arm around her.

The woman, who had struck Lani as a harsh schoolmistress type, seemed to soften. Her voice held a note of tenderness. "You look as though you are going to be sick. Let me get you some water." After setting her clipboard down, she hurried out of the room. Her heels clicked on the hard surface of the floor.

Noah snatched up the picture of Lani, holding it by the corner so as not to contaminate it too much. He flipped it over to where letters had been cut out of magazines.

Lani peered over his shoulder to read.

Say you love me or else.

The words sent a chill down her spine. Something about Noah standing close to her made the fear bearable.

He stared at the front again. "What a mixed message.

Find me some sort of bag to put it in. Maybe Forensics can come up with something on it."

Lani doubted it. The guy had been super careful so far. "Yes, and I think we better consult a psychologist to try and understand his motive. He's clearly not a stable human being."

The woman returned holding a paper cup. "Here you go, dear." The woman's whole demeanor had changed to become much more maternal. "Are you not feeling well?"

Lani took a sip of the water allowing the cool liquid to soothe her throat. She glanced up at Noah, finding strength in his gaze. There was no need to share with this woman everything that was going on. "I think we just need to get home. Do you have a plastic bag we could use?"

The woman disappeared again and returned with one. Lani appreciated that she didn't ask any questions.

Lani held her purse up. "Thank you for your trouble."

"I'll walk you two out," said the woman.

Noah placed a protective hand on Lani's back as they headed out to the hallway and down the stairs where the woman said goodbye to them.

"So what do you think that guy was planning?"

The question did not upset Lani. It had been reeling through her mind as well. "I think he saw that I was alone. He made noise on purpose to lure me into that room. He probably wanted to scare me by showing me the photo."

"But he panicked and ran," said Noah.

When they entered the wide hallway, a man in a waiter's uniform was moving from room to room shutting off the lights.

"Yeah, maybe he heard you coming up the stairs," Lani said. "You got to me pretty fast." She turned to face him for a moment to look into his green eyes. What did she see there? Affection? Admiration?

"I was worried about you." His voice filled with warmth. She liked the way his mouth curled up in the faintest smile. She hadn't noticed before that his eyes had gold flecks in them.

There was a lot she hadn't noticed about Noah before all this happened. He was the quiet, serious Jameson brother. Noah had an integrity and a depth of character that she admired. As she stared into his eyes, she had to be honest with herself. She was falling for him. Feelings that she had locked away in a box a year ago were coming alive.

"Last call, folks, we got to shut this place down." The man in the waiter's uniform turned off the hallway lights.

The waiter's interruption killed the power of the moment between them. Lifting her skirt, she turned. "I just need to get cleaned up a little bit."

Noah looked down at his torn pants. "Me too."

She turned back to face him. "If he wants me to say I love him, why doesn't he tell me how and when?" Her voice tinged with pain. "He said he would give Oscar back if I did." She couldn't bear the thought of anything bad happening to that dog.

"I think he gets some sort of sick thrill out of toying with you. It's about power and control," said Noah.

After both of them retreated to respective bathrooms to get cleaned up, they stepped outside into the darkness and headed toward the parking lot.

It had been a long night for both of them. Yet, there

was something about going through it all with Noah that she could get used to.

There was a small cluster of people still visiting in the parking lot. One of the men broke away from the group and headed toward them.

Noah spoke under his breath. "It's the deputy commissioner. I'm going to have to make nice." He grabbed her hand and squeezed it. "Help me out."

His touch lit a fire inside her. And she liked that he sought out her support.

The deputy commissioner was a tall African American man with a bright smile. "Noah, talk about running into you at the last minute." He held out his hand.

"Good to run into you, John." Noah shook John's hand and then turned toward Lani. "This is officer Lani Branson. She's with the NYC K-9 Command Unit and a close friend."

John offered Lani a nod and then turned his attention back to Noah. "I was actually hoping I'd see you tonight."

"Oh?" Noah drew his shoulders back ever so slightly, body language that to anyone else would have been unnoticeable. But Lani knew it meant he was nervous. They'd been spending so much time together she was starting to pick up on things like that.

The deputy commissioner continued. "Yes, I wanted to tell you what a great job you have been doing as chief. I know when we lost your brother, you stepped up as acting chief. The commissioner agrees that we want to offer you the position on a permanent basis."

"Noah, that's wonderful." Though her voice gave nothing away, Lani felt like she'd been knocked in the stomach. "What a great opportunity." She wanted to be happy for Noah, but if he took the job it truly meant they would only ever be friends.

"Thank you. I'll have to think about it," said Noah.

A woman in a pastel orange colored gown broke away from the group and came toward them. She touched John's arm in a way that indicated they were a couple. "Do we know how to close a party down or what? We should get going, John, we already owe the sitter a small fortune."

"Get back to me with your answer as soon as possible, Noah," the deputy commissioner said before he wrapped his arms around his wife's shoulder and walked toward one of the remaining cars.

Noah turned to face Lani. "Come on, I'll take you home."

Noah escorted her back to his car where he held the door for her. She sat in the passenger seat feeling numb. Of course, Noah should take the job as chief. Why was he even thinking about it?

For a moment, she'd let herself entertain the idea that maybe they could be more than friends if Noah went back to working patrol. She wasn't going to deny the feelings. She just didn't need to act on them and stand in the way of Noah getting ahead in his career.

"It's a great opportunity for you…to be the chief permanently." It felt like she was pulling the words up from the bottom of her toes.

"Sure," he said. He seemed very far away, lost in thoughts of his own.

They drove through the city. She watched the honey-colored headlights of other cars bleep by on the express-way as the hole inside her grew. The reality was that as much as she liked Noah, there could not be anything romantic between the two of them.

Noah slowed down as he turned onto the residential street that led to her house. He double-parked in front of her house. The glow of the lights inside indicated that Reed was home.

"I'll wait until you're inside," he said.

She pushed open the door.

"Thanks for helping me out tonight," said Noah. "I couldn't have done it without you."

"No problem. I had fun even with everything that happened." She slipped out of the car and turned back to face him. "It's what one friend does for another, right?"

He hesitated in answering. She could not read his expression in the dim light. "Yeah, sure," he said. His voice sounded a million miles away.

"You have a good night, what's left of it. Get some sleep." She shut the car door and headed up the walkway to her house feeling like she had been hollowed out on the inside. She could see Reed through the window watching television. Jessie lay on the couch resting her head on Reed's thigh. A welcome sight. Reed waved at her from inside the house.

She peered over her shoulder at Noah, who hadn't pulled away from the curb yet. She swung open the door and stepped inside, feeling as though something in her life had died.

ELEVEN

Noah watched as the last of Lani's martial arts students shuffled out of the dojo and headed toward the locker rooms. A few parents waited in chairs in the viewing area along with Noah and Scotty while others must have run errands and would pick up their ten-year-olds in a few minutes.

"Great class. See you next week," said Lani as she stood at the front of the room with her hands on her hips. She even looked great in a martial arts uniform. Her long blond ponytail set high on her head.

In the days since their night at the castle, things between them had seemed a little frosty. Lani had been pushing to be back out in the field, arguing that the stalker was going to get to her no matter what. Why did her training have to be stalled? The logic of the argument wasn't lost on him. She even wanted to know why she had to be stuck at a desk with him. Her saying that hurt. Didn't she like being around him? Or was it just the inactivity that was hard for her? Lani was a woman of action. Maybe her coldness had nothing to do with him and was just because she was so frustrated by the confinement and the need for protection.

Still, anytime Reed or one of the other officers was available, she'd chosen them over Noah to be her protection. That did feel personal. Tonight, none of the other officers were free, so he got to see her in action teaching her class. Lani was a natural teaching the kids using humor while still maintaining control.

Noah rose to help Lani put away some of the equipment. She handed him a spray bottle and a cloth. "You can sanitize the mats. I'll put this equipment away and then I got some paperwork I have to do in the office on the third floor."

"Take Scotty with you," he said.

"Sure, no problem." She offered him the faintest of smiles. She commanded Scotty to follow her and disappeared through a door which he assumed led to an office.

It wasn't that she was abrupt or even dismissive toward him, it was just that he could feel distance between them. He sprayed down the mats as the last of the parents drifted away and noise from the locker room died out.

He enjoyed the time he spent with her so much. And yes, he was attracted to her. He admired her compassion and her integrity. When he wasn't around her, he missed her easy laugh and animated storytelling.

He heard a door slam somewhere. His heart squeezed tight as concern for Lani's safety rose up in him. He dropped the spray bottle and hurried in the direction Lani had gone. The door led to a narrow set of stairs which Noah took two at a time. The building must have been a residence at one time, these narrow stairs for servants to travel up and down the floors without being intrusive.

The stairs led him to a door on the third floor that was slightly ajar. He pushed it open. Lani sat at a desk behind a computer. The room was the size of a broom closet. Uniforms and belts of various colors still in their packaging and a file cabinet took up most of the remaining space.

Lani looked up from her computer. Though Noah couldn't see him, Scotty must be on the other side of the desk in the tight quarters.

"Everything okay?" She glanced back at her screen.

The panic that had made his chest tight released its hold on him. "Yeah, I just thought I heard a door slam. Is anybody else in this building?"

"I wouldn't think so at this hour. There are two other tenants on the second floor. I think a bookkeeper and a guy who sells real estate. One of them might be working late."

"Maybe, I'll just have a look around," he said.

"I'll be done here in a few minutes. I've just got to get this letter about the tournament written and sent off," Lani said. She leaned over to pet Scotty. "We'll be fine here."

Noah stepped away from the threshold. "I'll let you know if anyone else is around." He headed down the hallway, opening doors. The office for the martial arts school and several rooms used for storage appeared to be the only thing on this top floor. He knew that the dojo and locker rooms took up all of the basement. But the building was laid out oddly and it wasn't obvious how to access the second floor. The narrow stairs that led to Lani's office had no other doors or exits. He returned to the dojo and found a second more substantial stairway on the other side of the building that led to the other offices.

Both the offices had signs on their doors indicating their respective businesses. He stood for a moment on the silent floor staring out the window at the city at night. Could the noise he'd heard just be a parent returning to grab some forgotten item? In and out so quickly he hadn't seen them?

He hurried back down the large stairway to the dojo. He peered in the now empty locker room and turned to head back up to where Lani and Scotty were.

An object hit the back of his head. Black dots filled his field of vision. He could feel his body falling forward in space as he crumpled face-first to the floor.

The last thought he had before the sensation that lights were being turned out and he was in total darkness was that maybe he should get up and make sure Lani was okay.

Lani finished the letter to the parents and hit the send button. She glanced down at Scotty. "Almost done here, buddy."

The dog looked at her and made a noise only Rottweilers made, somewhere between a groan and a whine. She rubbed the top of his head. "I miss you too, when I can't see you."

Scotty and Noah were sort of a package deal. If being around Noah was just too painful, it meant she didn't get to see the sweet Rottweiler either. She cared for Noah. Maybe it was just because of the danger they had faced together, but her connection to him was so deep. Knowing that they could never be anything more than friends made her feel like the heartache might overwhelm her when she was around him. Maybe that would change with time.

Having to work so closely with him in the confined space of his office put her over the top. She'd been pushing to get back out in the field for more reasons than just to continue her training.

Lani closed down the computer and bent over to get her purse. She rose to her feet and squeezed through the tiny space between the desk and the file cabinet pushing a chair out of the way to get through and then putting it back in place. Her back was to the door when she reached for her coat.

A hand went over her mouth as lips pressed close to her ears. "Now I have you all to myself."

She pulled his hand away from her mouth, but the man's grip around her waist was like iron. "I love you. Are you happy?" She spoke through gritted teeth. "Where is Oscar?"

Her attacker squeezed her even tighter making it hard to breath. "You sound so sincere." He wrapped the arm that had been over her mouth around her, so her neck was in the crook of his elbow.

Scotty jumped up putting his front paws on the desk, going ballistic with his barking. The desk was not one he could slip under to have access to her attacker. Lani had had to move a chair to even let him in behind the desk. Now that chair blocked him.

The man's anaconda-like grip weakened for just a moment. He probably hadn't counted on Scotty being here. Scotty's intense barking filled the tiny space. In the second that the attacker was distracted, Lani tore away from him and turned to face the man who had made her a prisoner.

She saw his face clearly for just a moment before he whirled to run. The arched eyebrows and gaunt features stood in sharp contrast to his muscular body. Now that face would be etched in her memory. Scotty had worked his way around the desk through the same tight space Lani had squeezed through. His paws tapped out an intense rhythm and scratched the linoleum as he made a beeline for the attacker who stepped toward the door and the narrow stairway.

Lani hurried after the dog. The attacker reached the bottom of the stairs in the basement and ran through the dojo. The dog continued the chase, but Lani stopped when she saw Noah lying facedown on the floor just outside the locker room. Her panic ratcheted up a notch at the sight of him not moving.

Knowing that Scotty would go after the attacker, she kneeled to check on Noah. He was unresponsive when she shook his shoulder. Fear washed through her as she rolled him over. His chest moved up and down. She let out a sharp breath. He was alive, but unconscious.

Above her on the second floor, Scotty's bark intensified and then she heard a yipping sound. A door slammed. Had the man been able to get away? She raced up the stairs on the other side of the dojo that led to the second floor and out to the street.

She found Scotty hurling himself at a shut door.

Noah called to her from the bottom of the stairs as he came around the corner. "Did he get away?"

She glanced down at him. He appeared a little wobbly on his feet. His hair was disheveled. His unfocused gaze suggested he hadn't fully recovered.

"Not yet." She swung open the door. Scotty burst through it giving chase. "He hasn't gotten away. Not if we can help it." She hurried after the dog who had stopped to sniff the ground and then took off running up an alley.

Scotty turned a corner. She couldn't see the dog anymore, but she could hear him.

Rain drizzled out of the dark sky. From the look of the shine on the street, it had been raining for some time. She slowed a little in her step, fearing an ambush from her attacker hiding behind something.

Noah came up behind her and touched her shoulder.

She pointed. "He went that way." With Scotty and Noah close by, she didn't fear being kidnapped or worse.

They sprinted up the alley and turned the corner. The street led to an open area. She could just make out Scotty as he raced toward a dark street. Noah lagged behind, probably still recovering from his injury. The attacker must have knocked Noah out so nothing would stop him from getting to Lani. But the stalker hadn't counted on Scotty.

The Rottweiler reached the street just as a single headlight came on. A motorcycle pulled away from the curb. Scotty chased after it, running for several blocks before the attacker gained enough speed to escape. His taillight faded in the distance.

Noah caught up with her and then ran out to get Scotty.

Feeling a sense of defeat, Lani shivered from being cold and wet. There hadn't been time to grab her coat. Noah returned with Scotty heeling beside him.

She reached out to stroke the dog's head. "You did good, boy." She gazed toward Noah, unable to read his expression in the darkness. He probably felt the same level of frustration she was experiencing. "Come on back inside, let's get dried off and warmed up."

The three of them trailed back toward the dark building. Once inside, Lani gathered up some clean towels from the locker room. They toweled off Scotty before drying their own hair and clothes. Her shirt was still damp from the rain, but she wasn't shivering.

"Come on up to the office. I'll make us some tea to warm up before we go," she said.

They trudged up the narrow, twisted stairs. Lani made the tea a cup at a time with the Keurig that rested on top of the file cabinet. She sat behind the desk and Noah sat on the desk since there was no room for another chair even if they had one. Scotty perched on the threshold of the door, exhausted from his run but still vigilant.

Noah blew on his steaming mug. "I'm sorry I let you down."

Lani scooted her chair back from her desk. "What do you mean?"

Noah touched the back of his head. "I was supposed to protect you, and that guy got the better of me."

"He didn't hurt me thanks to Scotty."

The dog let out a huff of air.

"I just wish we could have caught him," said Noah.

"I did get a look at him." Lani bit her lip as the memory of her attacker's face materialized in her head. "I can tell you for sure that he's not a former boyfriend or anyone I arrested. Still, it feels like I've seen him somewhere."

Noah took a gulp of tea. "That's progress. We can have you look through some databases or put together a police sketch." He set his mug on the desk.

Lani finished her tea and set the mugs aside. She could wash them next time she was teaching a class. "You ready to take me home?"

Noah rose to his feet. "Yes, let's go."

Scooting the chair to one side, Lani squeezed through the narrow space between desk and file cabinet.

Noah grabbed her coat from where it hung on a hook. He placed it over her shoulders, and she slipped her arms through the sleeves. He stepped out first so she would have room to stand on the landing and face him.

Scotty rose and moved closer to the stairs.

She stared up into his green eyes. "This is getting old."

He shook his head.

She sighed. "Sometimes it just feels like this is never going to end. That I will be at this guy's mercy forever. Being escorted around."

He leaned toward her. "It hasn't been awful, has it? Being with me." His face lit up with that soft smile.

Here they were again, looking into each other's eyes. She wondered if he was experiencing the same magnetic pull toward her that she felt to him. She wished he would put his hand on her cheek. She wanted to be held in his arms. She longed to feel his touch.

She cleared her throat and took a step back. "No, it hasn't been terrible." *Just heartbreaking at times.* "I enjoy your company, Noah." Lost in the moment, she struggled to tear her gaze from his face.

Scotty whined and wagged his tail. Noah looked away, brushing his hand over the dog's back. "Okay, buddy, let's take this lady home."

They took the stairs to the second floor and out onto the street. Noah had parked the car several blocks away. They passed only a few people on the sidewalk. This wasn't a part of Queens with a lot of nightlife.

After loading Scotty in the back, Noah opened the

passenger side door. "You should probably drive since I was just hit on the head." He tossed her the keys.

Lani got behind the wheel.

Scotty must have sensed the heaviness of the moment. He rested his chin on the seat and made his I'm-here-for-you noise. As Lani pulled out onto the street, Noah reached back and patted Scotty's jaw.

The moment of intense attraction she'd felt back at the office weighed on her. She needed to know what was to be between them. "So have you decided about becoming the chief permanently?" As much as she dreaded the answer, the question had to be asked.

Noah answered. "I suppose the deputy commissioner will want an answer soon. Being with you has given me a chance to spend more time in the field. I do miss it after nearly seven months of mostly sitting at a desk."

Her heart fluttered. So he wasn't sold on the idea of taking the promotion. "Yeah, desk duty makes me restless."

A few blocks later, he spoke up. "It's a tough choice. Lot to think about."

She smoothed her hand over her shirt and stared out through the windshield. The city ticked by in her peripheral vision, dark office buildings, neon, people spilling into the street from restaurants and bars.

Lani took the exit that led to her house. They rode the remaining way in silence. She circled the block until a space opened up close to her house.

Lani grabbed the door handle. "You should make sure there is nothing seriously wrong with your head."

"I should be okay. I'll go in tomorrow."

She turned back to look at him. Light from a streetlamp

spilled into the car. She could see the brightness in his eyes and his angular features.

"Don't be bummed about the guy getting away tonight. Being able to ID him is a big step toward catching him."

Lani felt like a balloon that all the air had been let out of. So he thought the reason for her silence was she was thinking about the stalker. "Yeah, hopefully he'll be behind bars soon." She stepped out to the curb and shoved her hands in her pockets. "So I can get on with my life." She shut the door and headed toward her house.

As always, she knew Noah would remain parked until she was safely inside. She glanced toward the street. The cab was still lit up, and Noah had slid into the driver's seat. She could see him as he held his phone to his ear.

She opened the door of her house. Maybe she had read the situation all wrong. The attraction only went one way.

Noah answered his phone. The number came up as his brother Carter.

"What's up, little brother?"

"Where you been? I keep hoping to catch you at home."

Carter sounded anxious. "I've been busy with work and…things." Like being a bodyguard for Lani. It seemed that anytime Noah was home Carter was sleeping.

"I was just wondering if anything new has come up with Jordan's murder," Carter said. "I figured it would cross your desk first."

Carter had not been on active duty for some months

since being shot in the knee. He was doing physical therapy and receiving temporary disability. The injury had been severe enough that the prognosis for Carter coming back on the force was not good. Being out of commission meant Carter had a lot of time to think and worry about Jordan's murder going so cold it was forgotten.

"Nothing new, Carter," said Noah. "'Preciate you checking in." There was a lot going unsaid with Carter's phone call. His call was a way of saying none of the brothers would let this case go cold. Any thread, any morsel of a clue had to be followed up on.

"Okay, thanks, big brother," Carter said. "Keep me in the loop if anything does surface. I have time now. I can make some calls and inquiries in an unofficial way. I'll let you know if I find anything that needs a more official follow-up."

"Can do," said Noah, a note of sorrow echoed through his words, for what Carter was going through with this injury and for the whole Jameson clan.

He glanced at Reed and Lani's brightly lit living room.

From the backseat, Scotty rested his chin on Noah's shoulder. "I know, boy. I like Lani a lot too."

He still wasn't sure what he wanted to do. He missed working the street and being in the field with Scotty and he liked working with Lani. If he stepped down as chief, maybe there could be something more than a friendship between them. If she had the same feelings for him as he was starting to have for her. That was a big if. He'd never been very good at reading women. Criminals he did fine with, but women were a mystery.

He stared at his phone. He could do a lot of good for

Lani and the other K-9 officers as the chief. And really he only trusted himself to make sure Jordy's case remained front and center. He felt the heaviness of his responsibilities, and then the memory of Lani's smile flashed through his head. Another time, another place it would be so easy to fall for her. He stroked Scotty's head. "Not everything can be about me or you and what we want. No matter how bad we want it."

Scotty licked the side of his face.

As he pulled away from the curb, he knew that the right decision would be to accept the permanent position as chief.

TWELVE

K-9 officer Tony Knight slapped Noah on the back as he unloaded Scotty from the patrol car.

"So it's all hands on deck," said Tony as his dog Rusty, a chocolate Lab, remained standing and alert. Rusty was trained in search and rescue, but with the Columbus Day Parade about to start, all the K-9s who weren't marching in the parade were on duty.

"Looks that way," said Noah. Scotty jumped out of his kennel in the back of the patrol car and stood at attention.

Up Fifth Avenue, Noah could hear the sound of a marching band warming up. Crowds were already lining the street in preparation for the parade, some of them waving Italian flags. From the police marching band to the motorcycle brigade, NYPD would be well represented. Several of the K-9s would be marching as well with the rest of law enforcement, but most of the K-9s would be on patrol. It would be a long day. Even after the parade, the celebrations would go on into the night in Little Italy. The day had come to be a celebration of Italian culture more than anything.

Another patrol car pulled up. Brianne got out of the

driver's seat and moved to the back of the vehicle to get Stella. Lani emerged from the passenger seat, walking around the vehicle toward Noah and Tony.

"What are you doing here?" said Noah.

"I think you could use every hand you've got. The pickpockets will be out in full force," said Lani. "For starters. We all know the crime level ticks up during this kind of event."

Scotty wagged his tail as Lani drew close. With Sophie back from her honeymoon, Lani had been on desk duty with a different department and spending time in the training facility working with the dogs. Like the rest of the K-9 unit, she had received the news of his acceptance as permanent chief at the morning briefing between shift changes. As Noah had stood at the front of the room to make the announcement, he saw her expression change. What was that he saw in tightened features? Concern? Anger? Maybe even disappointment. After the briefing, he had meant to find her, but she'd disappeared while the other officers were slapping his back and shaking his hand. Since then, she'd made herself scarce. He'd seen her only in passing and there was no time to talk. He missed her.

Lani was right that the presence of the dogs tended to cut down on the muggings and pickpockets. Lani's keen eyes and athletic ability might come in handy too.

She reached down to pet Scotty. "The stalker finds a way to get to me no matter what. I wanted to be a help. I'm used to action and activity, Noah. Desk duty is going to make me feel claustrophobic."

She was right on that account too. Desk duty hadn't kept her safe.

"Okay," said Noah. "Stay close to me."

"Ten-four," said Lani.

The dissonant sound of marching bands warming up grew louder. Several blocks up Fifth Avenue he could see a large balloon of a cartoon character floating in the air. The people lined up ten deep on the sidewalk up to the street where barriers had been set up. This part of Fifth Avenue was one of the places entertainers in the parade would stop to perform.

Brianne and Tony headed south while he and Lani took the other side of the street. The crowd parted for them as Scotty trotted through. Some of the kids wanted to pet Scotty, which Noah allowed. Having the dogs out with all these people provided a PR opportunity.

Lani's shoulder brushed against his. Her presence had a debilitating effect on him and her touch turned his knees to mush. That he had that sort of a reaction when he was close to her, he would just have to accept and keep in check.

The sound of the approaching parade grew even louder as people pressed toward the edge of the street in anticipation.

Lani nodded her head toward a teenage boy who had stepped back away from the crowd toward the store-fronts. His eyes grew wide at the sight of Lani and Noah.

"Something is up with that kid," said Lani. "I think he lifted a wallet."

Scotty quickened his pace. The teenager turned to run, a sign that he was up to something. Lani sprinted after him. The side streets were virtually abandoned. Noah could see her blond head as she burst down the alley after the suspect. Scotty bounded ahead. Noah led him down a side street in an effort to cut the suspect off once he emerged from the alley.

Scotty bolted to the edge of the alley and barked.

Lani stood at the other end of the alley with her hand hovering over her gun. She didn't see any sign that he had a weapon, but training taught her to never assume.

The kid raised his arms. "I didn't do anything. Make that dog stop barking at me."

"I saw you ditch the wallet back there," said Lani. "And I saw you take it from the man in front of you."

"Okay," said the kid.

Noah gave Scotty the command to stop barking and sit. The kid still watched the dog closely with an expression of fright on his face.

"Why don't we walk back to where you dropped the wallet. You can give it back to the man and apologize," said Noah.

The jails were going to be full before the day was over. Taking this kid in would be pointless.

The kid shrugged, glanced at Scotty and then trudged back up the alley. Noah stepped in behind the suspect, keeping Scotty's lead short. The kid acted like he was going to cooperate as long as Scotty was around. Dogs were effective in that way. The teenage boy stopped to root beside a dumpster for the stolen wallet.

Though they were several blocks from the action, the noise of the parade swelled to a crescendo as the first of the marchers went by and the crowd cheered.

On command, Scotty sat while the teen continued to search for the wallet behind the dumpster.

Noah glanced over at Lani who was studying the fire escapes and windows of the apartment building. Was she always wondering if she was being watched?

Even though they had a face to go with her stalker, the search through the databases of criminals had yielded no results. The guy must not have a criminal history. He hadn't had time to find out if Lani had sat down with the police sketch artist.

When she caught him staring, she lowered her gaze and tilted her head to one side, shaking it a little, probably meaning that she was thinking about the stalker, but that she didn't notice anything that indicated the stalker was around. The connection between them was so strong, no words needed to be exchanged.

It was the kind of connection that made two people good partners as police officers, but he had a feeling it ran even deeper than that.

"Here it is. I found it." The teenager stood up waving a wallet.

Noah took the wallet. "Do you remember what the man you took it off of looked like?"

"From behind. He had on a red jacket." The kid stared at the ground. Returning the wallet and apologizing would probably be punishment enough.

Lani came to stand beside Noah. Noah opened up the wallet and showed the kid and Lani the driver's license. "That's who we're looking for."

When they reached the street where the parade was passing by, the number of spectators had grown even more.

Noah with Scotty in tow hung close to the teenager while he searched for the wallet's owner. The crowd always gave wide berth to Scotty.

"There." The teen pointed to a man in a red jacket.

They pressed through the crowd. The boy tapped the man in the red jacket on the shoulder and made his apologies when the man turned around. Noah handed him his wallet.

The man glanced at Noah and then back at the teen, whose tight features and stiff shoulders indicated he was distraught.

"I don't need to press charges," said the man.

The teen melted with relief. His shoulders and his expression softened, and he disappeared into the crowd.

Noah glanced up expecting to see Lani. All he saw was a sea of faces all focused on the passing parade. Panic gripped him. Had the stalker found a way to get to her? He and Scotty squeezed through the crowd, searching. He pushed toward the storefronts still not seeing her.

When he caught sight of the back of Lani's head, he let out the breath he was holding. Even though he'd lost her in the crowd for only minutes, the feeling that something bad might have happened to her and she would no longer be in his life, made him see how much he cared about her.

He rushed toward her. She slipped deeper into the crowd. A wall of people came in front of her and he lost sight of her.

He called out her name. Where was she going? Scotty walked in front of him, parting the crowd. He caught a glimpse of her blond head now half a block away.

He hurried toward her, wondering what had caught her attention.

Though she was shaking with fear, Lani squeezed her way through the throngs of people. She'd seen her stalker, and he had Oscar. She looked over her shoulder hoping to see Noah and Scotty. There hadn't been time to let him know what was going on. She dared not even slow down to radio him.

The man had grinned at her in the most sinister way while he held the puppy, and then he'd been swallowed up by the crowd. She'd probably lost him, but more than anything she wanted to get Oscar back. She doubted he would hurt her as long as she remained where people were.

She hurried around a group of children. The crowd thinned. Up the side street, she saw Oscar's head bobbing as he was pulled on a leash. She saw the back of the man and then he was gone again around a corner.

Someone touched her shoulder.

She whirled around. All the fear left her tense body when she saw that it was Noah.

"Oscar. I saw Oscar."

"Are you sure it was Oscar. There are a lot of yellow Labs in this city."

"He was with the man I saw at the studio. They just went around the corner."

Noah tugged on Scotty's leash. "Let's go." Noah's walk intensified to a jog. "I'm glad I caught up with you. He's probably setting a trap."

They hurried up the street. A few parade watchers were lined up for a half a block on the side street. They broke free of the crowd. Despite street closures due to the parade, there were still people wandering around. None of them had a yellow Lab puppy.

Lani scanned the entire area not seeing the dog or the man. They continued up the street. She heard a faint bark, Oscar's bark.

"He's headed toward the subway," she said.

They hurried toward the stairs that led to the subway.

Noah clicked on his radio. "Got a suspect with the missing yellow Lab headed down the Fifty-Ninth Street entrance. Officer Branson and I are in pursuit."

They hurried down the stairs. Noah flashed his badge and leapt over the turnstile. The platform was busy but not overly crowded. She scanned the sea of faces. It wouldn't be that easy to hide a squirmy yellow Lab.

Noah patted her shoulder. "Scotty and I will check that area around the corner."

Lani hurried up and down the platform searching. Her radio glitched. She clicked her on button. "Go ahead."

The voice was Tony's. "Rusty and I are at the exit. No sign of him."

"Nothing here either. Will continue the search." Lani peered over her shoulder at where Noah had gone behind her. No sign of Noah. "Our suspect is wearing a blue jacket and a baseball hat."

"Got it," said Tony. "I read your description of him in the report you filed. Muscular guy."

She hurried past some buskers playing guitar and violin. She could hear the subway moving through the tunnel whizzing toward the platform. She scanned the crowd again. If the man was in hiding, he might step out to board the subway. Her heart pounded in her chest. He was here somewhere. He had to be.

Up ahead, she saw Tony and his chocolate Lab. When she glanced over her shoulder, Noah had emerged from around the corner. He shook his head. The stalker must know that he was trapped. Where was he hiding?

Screams rose up from the crowd gathering to board the subway. Lani turned one way and then the other, trying to figure out what had caused the panic. The attention of the crowd was directed toward the tracks.

All the air left her lungs when she saw Oscar bounding along the tracks, stopping to sniff something on the ground. The sound of the approaching train pressed on her ears. Lani sprinted toward the tracks to the edge of the platform. Scotty ran out ahead of her and leaped down onto the tracks. Scotty hurried after Oscar and grabbed him by the collar. The weight of the six-month-old pup looked to be almost too much for Scotty to carry.

The train was within seconds of arriving at the platform. Scotty reached the area between track and platform. Lani sprinted the distance to where the dog was at. She reached down and gathered Oscar in her arms.

The sound of the approaching train filled the tunnel. Noah came out of nowhere. All her attention had been on Oscar. Noah jumped down on the tracks and boosted Scotty back on the platform. Lani reached an arm down to help Noah up just as the train came into view. Though it had slowed to make the stop, Noah lay on the platform only seconds before it whizzed past and came to a stop.

A cheer rose up from the crowd. Noah shifted from being on his stomach to sitting. Lani gasped for air while Oscar crawled into her lap.

The doors of the subway slid open.

Still out of breath, Lani bolted to her feet. "He'll use this chance to get away. He probably wanted Oscar to be a distraction."

Noah rose to his feet as well. "Looks like Tony's got the train covered."

Lani glanced down the platform to see Tony and his dog board the subway.

Lani grabbed the leash that was still attached to Oscar. She searched all the boarding passengers and then turned her attention to the people who remained. None looked like her stalker. None bolted for the exit to indicate their guilt. Maybe Tony and Rusty would find him.

Noah patted her shoulder. "He must have slipped out when we were saving Oscar."

Lani nodded. She leaned down to gather Oscar into her arms. "I'm glad I have this little guy back." Oscar licked her face.

"Scotty and I will do one more search up and down," Noah said.

Lani trailed behind pulling the easily distracted Oscar along. The pup stopped to wag his tail at a group of girls in school uniforms. The girls oohed and aahed. Oscar knew how to turn on the charm. Her phone beeped that she had a text. She clicked open the message.

The dog was too much trouble. Next time it will be your boyfriend.

Before, the message might have sent a wave of fear through her. But she was stronger now.

Noah came back over to her. "He got away. I'm sure of it." He stepped a little closer toward her. "Is something wrong?"

"Another message from him." She lifted the phone up so he could take it and read the text.

"That guy has some nerve." Noah's forehead crinkled as he shook his head. He turned his attention to

Oscar. "The good news is, sometimes being an obnoxious puppy works in your favor."

Oscar yipped and bounced around Lani's feet.

"Who does he mean, 'your boyfriend'? I thought you weren't dating anyone."

"He must assume it's you since we're together so much," Lani said. "I'm sure if someone were watching from a distance, it might appear that way."

He shrugged. "I guess so."

Tony's voice came through Noah's radio. "We got nothing here. Sorry."

Noah radioed back. "Nothing here either."

"Well, guess we better finish the shift," she said. "I'll put Oscar in your car if that's all right."

"Yeah, I'm sure the celebration will be going on into the night in Little Italy." Noah let go of the radio and straightened his neck to look at Lani. "The Jamesons have their own Columbus Day celebration. Lots of Italian food. You want to come?" His eyes rested on her for a long moment. "Reed is welcome to come along."

Lani felt torn. She missed spending time with Noah, but being around him brought up the pain that there could never be anything between them.

"My mom makes an awesome lasagna." He tried to entice her.

"Can't turn that down, can I?"

"Great, let's go up topside and finish out this shift. Parade has probably moved past, but I'm sure there are still plenty of opportunists working the crowd."

They stepped toward the subway exit and climbed up into the daylight, Lani wrestling with the uncertainty of everything in her life. Could she handle just being

Noah's friend? Would she be able to complete her training with the stalker still out there?

The only thing she knew for sure was that she was glad to have Oscar back. Even if he wasn't police dog material, she'd grown fond of the little guy.

THIRTEEN

Noah lifted the lid on the spaghetti sauce and took in a deep breath filled with oregano and basil. His mouth watered. He reached for a spoon to sample the sauce. As he drew the spoon up to his mouth, he breathed in the heady aroma again.

His mother entered the kitchen. "Get out of there. If you boys keep sampling the food, there will be nothing left for dinner."

His mother tended toward exaggeration. She had cooked enough to feed an army. Ivy Jameson's blue eyes held a sparkle that had faded a little since the death of her son. Her dark hair was pulled up in a topknot. Even though she dressed in jeans and a blouse, she always carried herself with a certain elegance.

Noah licked his lips and put the spoon down. "It could use just a smidgen more garlic."

Ivy wagged a finger at her son. "Too many cooks spoil the soup, and the same could be said of spaghetti sauce. Now go on back into the living room. I'm sure your guest will be here any minute. What did you say her name was?"

"Lani."

"Yes, I've met her. Pretty girl, blonde. Nice lady." Her voice dropped half an octave and she gazed out the window. "I remember her from Jordan's funeral." Ivy studied her son for a moment. The jovial tone returned to her voice. "You like her, don't you? I noticed you cleaned up and put on a fresh shirt."

"Can't a guy take a shower without being accused of ulterior motives?" said Noah.

Ivy laughed and shook her head while she stirred the sauce and checked the lasagna in the oven. "I know my son."

Noah rested his hand on the counter. "Okay, I like her...as a friend. I'm her direct supervisor, so nothing is going to happen."

"Too bad. Your brothers have all met such nice women."

"I know, Mom. One of us has to be the forever bachelor, right?"

Ivy shut the oven door and placed her hand on her hip. She reached over and squeezed Noah's chin. "I want you to meet a nice girl. If not Lani, then maybe one of those sweet women from the Sunday school class your father and I teach."

It was his turn to stare out the window. "Yeah, maybe." The phrase "if not Lani" echoed through his head. The truth was he had dated a couple of the women from church. All of them were nice, but kind of ordinary.

The doorbell rang. By the time Noah made it into the living room, his niece Ellie had answered the door. Ellie was Carter's daughter by his first wife who had died. His brother Zach sat on the couch with his wife, Violet. Carter and his fiancée, Rachelle, stood by the window watching the dogs play outside through the sliding glass door. And Katie, Jordan's widow, sat by herself. Her tunic length blouse covered her bulging belly. The family had learned of her pregnancy after Jordan's death.

Alexander, the family patriarch, rested in his easy chair, arms folded over his chest, half dozing. He wore a Mets sweatshirt and baggy pants.

Ellie opened the door. Lani stood holding a casserole dish. Her brother, Reed, was behind her. Katie pushed herself to her feet. "Let me take that."

As the two women stood by each other, he was struck by how much they looked alike. Both were blonde, similar hairstyles, tall and slender.

"It's my contribution to the festivities. Just some brownies. Not very Italian, I know."

Noah was impressed that she'd managed to throw anything together in the short time they'd gotten off shift.

Zach rose to his feet. "All the food in this house gets eaten." He held a hand out to Lani. "Good to see you. I've been in the field so much. I guess our paths haven't crossed much lately."

"Yeah, Noah pretty much has me at a desk for now," Lani said.

A little tension entered the room. Of course, his brothers knew about the stalker. But they had a rule about not bringing work into family celebrations. Noah diverted the conversation to the Mets.

Lani and Reed stepped into the living room. The group engaged in small talk until Ivy called them all to the large dining room table which overflowed with food. Zach opened the sliding glass door so the dogs could come in. Frosty, Eddie and Scotty lay down just on the threshold between living room and kitchen. The two foster pups of Stella, one black and one yellow, whom Carter referred to as Mutt and Jeff pranced around the older dogs before settling down.

After Alexander said grace, dishes were passed around and plates filled up with food. The conversation was about the parade, which Ellie had attended with Carter and Rachelle.

Lani shared about getting Oscar back.

"So where is he now?" Zach asked.

"He's back at the kennels for now. The vet is making sure he wasn't harmed while he was being held. I know he needs to be returned to his foster family. I just am fond of the little guy. He's not K-9 material."

Reed laughed. "Yeah, he's kind of hyper. He gives Jessie a run for her money. She's not used to that kind of energy."

Lani tore apart a piece of garlic bread. "Speaking of missing dogs. Have you made any progress in finding Snapper? I was thinking you should look on the website I checked when I was trying to find Oscar."

Noah glanced nervously at Katie. Lani didn't know they didn't talk police business at meals. He tensed, worried that bringing up anything about Jordan's death would be upsetting to Katie this late in her pregnancy. Snapper was his brother's K-9 who had gone missing after Jordan's murder.

Reed shook his head. "No progress far as I know even with that sketch Dominic helped us put together of the man who gave Snapper to Dominic."

Katie set her glass down. "There was a sketch made of the man who took Snapper?"

Noah glanced at his brothers, feeling a rising tension. Dominic was a foster kid from Brooklyn who'd taken care of Snapper for a while before the dog had run off. Dominic claimed that a man had given him the German shepherd, and everyone hoped that finding the guy would result in Jordy's murderer being put behind bars. Reed and his fiancée, Abigail, were working on adopting Dominic. "We weren't trying to keep you out of the loop, Katie."

"We just wanted to protect you and your baby," said Carter.

Lani cleared her throat. "I'm sorry. I think I may have spoken out of turn."

Noah placed a hand over hers. "You had no way of knowing."

Katie sat across the table from Noah. She put her napkin on the table. "I want to see that sketch." She rested a protective hand on her stomach.

"I can probably pull it up on my computer after we eat."

Alex raised his glass of lemonade. "Yes, later. Now let's enjoy the meal."

Noah glanced at Carter and then at Zach. Katie had a right to know what was going on with the investigation, but with the baby due in three weeks, he didn't want to add stress to her life.

After dinner, Noah went upstairs to retrieve his laptop. He sat on the back porch watching the dogs play while Katie and Lani leaned in close to see his screen. The trees had turned shades of gold, rust and yellow and a cool autumn breeze whirled around them. They all had put on their fall jackets while they sipped the cider Ivy had offered them.

Noah typed in his password to access the official

files. He clicked past a long list of documents before the sketch came up on-screen.

Katie sat back in a lawn chair. Her voice grew cold. "I know who that is."

Breath caught in his throat. This could be the breakthrough they needed to catch Jordy's killer. Noah glanced at Lani.

"Can I have a closer look?" Lani asked.

Noah handed her the laptop and then drew his attention to Katie.

Noah tilted his head toward the computer. "So who is he?"

Katie rose to her feet and stepped to the edge of the porch. "His name is Martin Fisher. I knew him from church. We dated briefly before I met Jordan. I hadn't seen him at church in ages. But he came to Jordan's funeral and gave his condolences."

So this Martin Fisher might have killed Jordy out of jealousy.

"What did he seem like at the funeral?" Noah stood up and stepped closer to Katie, who gripped the railing of the porch. "I'm sorry I have to ask you these questions."

"It's all right. If this will get us closer to catching Jordan's killer—" she turned to face her brother-in-law "—I don't mind thinking about it." She smoothed her hand over her belly. "The two of us will be all right."

"Did he act peculiar in any way?"

She shook her head. "He was perfectly nice. And seemed really concerned about me." Katie looked down at the ground, still resting her hand on her tummy. "He came by about three weeks ago to check in on me. He wanted to take me out to dinner. I said I wasn't ready to date."

"How did he react to that? Was he angry?"

Katie shook her head. "One of the reasons we only went out a couple of times was that he came on a little strong, in kind of a smothering way. When I turned him down three weeks ago, I could tell he was upset, but he was still polite."

"Can you tell us anything else about him?"

"We only went out a couple of times. He worked construction and stayed in good shape for that."

Katie turned back toward the house, shaking her head. "Why would Martin have taken Snapper? You don't think…"

Her voice trailed off, but Noah knew what she was thinking. Was Martin Jordan's killer? It looked that way. But he could not draw a conclusion without solid evidence. Still, this felt like a huge step in the right direction. Noah shook his head. "I don't know anything for sure."

Ivy opened the sliding glass doors. "Come on inside, people. We've got gelato and Lani's brownies." Ivy closed the door and disappeared back into the kitchen.

"I think I might need to lie down for a bit," said Katie. "If there is any progress in the case, I want to know from now on, okay?"

He nodded. His sister-in-law went inside to head up the stairs.

Noah shook his head. He hated putting her through all this, but she was a strong woman. If they had kept her in the loop in the first place, they would have been able to ID the man in the sketch sooner.

He turned back to face Lani who had closed the laptop. Her features were taut. And her face had gone pale.

She tapped her finger on the laptop. "I think this is the same man who has been after me."

Noah reeled from the confusion. "But how?"

"I barely glanced at the sketch when it was shown in a briefing. We look at half a dozen of those a week. But now that I look at it and his face is burned in my mind... I think it's the same guy."

Noah sat down beside her. "If his connection is to Katie, why is he after you?"

"I don't know either. We kind of look alike. Katie said he was a little over-the-top with his affection when they were dating."

"Like he is using you as some kind of substitute." Katie and Lani were both blonde and blue-eyed, but their personalities were miles apart. Katie was quiet and thoughtful and Lani was outgoing and talkative. Noah stared at the sky. "I think we need to talk to a psychologist. I'm going to get a patrol unit to go to Martin Fisher's last known address right away."

"I agree. I'm with Katie that I want this all to be over with. Not just for me but for her."

Noah could feel his body tense from all the questions that hung in the air. Martin connected to Katie and he'd had Jordan's dog at one point. Did that mean Martin had killed Jordan? The evidence wasn't in yet, but he clearly had motive if he thought Jordan's death would help him be with Katie. But why bring Lani into it?

Lani walked up and down the hallway of the commercial high-rise searching for the address Noah had given her. They had agreed to meet Dr. Brenda Bench-

ley, a private psychologist who often consulted with the
police. It was Lani's day off and Noah had taken a long
lunch to meet her here.

His text had come in a moment earlier saying he
was delayed.

And now she couldn't find the office. Martin Fisher
was still at large. Officers had been dispatched to his
last known address as soon as they had his name, but
Martin's landlord said he'd moved out three weeks ago.

Half the building was undergoing a remodel. Plastic was drawn across some side corridors and she could
hear the sound of tools being used and men barking orders and questions at each other.

Her heart squeezed tight. Katie had said that Martin
was a construction worker. Of course, that didn't mean
he was here. She took in a breath to calm herself.

A man drew one of the plastic curtains aside and
stepped out.

It wasn't Martin. But she had tensed all the same.

The man had dark hair that was graying at the tem-
ples. "Lady, are you lost?" He rested his hand on his
tool belt.

"I'm trying to find an office." She showed him the
address on her phone.

"Don't know it."

"It belongs to a psychologist."

Light came into the man's face and he nodded.
"That's up a floor. You must have her old address. She
moved her office when all the remodeling started."

Lani thanked the man, who disappeared behind the
plastic curtain. She headed toward the door marked
Stairs, walking slowly so she could text Noah about
the change of address. She heard footsteps behind her

but when she looked up and turned around, no one was there. Her heart beat a little faster. She searched the area, which had connecting hallways where someone could have gone. The corridors appeared to be unoccupied.

Maybe the stairwell wasn't such a good idea. She searched for the elevator and got on. Lani found the psychologist's office which had "Dr. Benchley" typed on a piece of paper and taped to the door.

A receptionist with short candy apple–red hair and cat-eye glasses looked up from her computer. "Yes?"

"I'm here to see Dr. Benchley, but I'm waiting for someone." She found a chair and sat down and tried to take in a deep breath. She hated the way Martin Fisher had a hold on her mind even if she couldn't prove he was around.

When Noah walked through the door, she could feel the tension leave her body and the air fill her lungs. His warm smile was a nice bonus.

"Sorry I couldn't get away faster," he said.

"Just through that door," said the receptionist.

Lani had always thought of herself as a free spirit and an independent woman. The only other men who made her feel safe when she was around them were her brother and her father.

She pushed open the door. Dr. Benchley sat at her desk with her laptop open. "Noah, it's always good to see you. Both of you have a seat." The doctor was maybe in her fifties. Her voice was soft, and she had a grand-motherly quality about her.

She closed her laptop. "So Noah explained the situation to me over the phone. It sounds to me like Martin Fisher may have a sort of transference taking place, and that's why he's been stalking you."

"But his attraction is toward Katie," Lani said.

The doctor shrugged. "Obsession is a funny thing. Maybe he sees her as unattainable. The fact that he has been both violent toward you and done things that suggest romantic attraction is what intrigues me the most. He can't acknowledge that Katie rejected him, but he has anger about that. Katie is sacred, untouchable, so he takes his anger out on you."

The doctor rose to her feet and put her hands in her pockets. "He may also not be able to process the rejection. He might have some sort of rich fantasy life that he and Katie are in a relationship. When reality creeps in, he feels anxious and he takes it out on you. I couldn't tell you for sure until I question him."

In the days since they had a name to go with the face, Noah had kept Lani in the loop about the challenge of trying to bring Martin in. It was too much to hope for just a simple arrest. The man had made himself all but invisible.

"We know he moved out of his place three weeks ago." Noah added, "Three weeks ago was also when he lost his job for giving the receptionist at the construction company unwanted attention."

"So the job loss might have triggered the instability into high gear," said Brenda.

Lani cleared her throat. "That's when the attacks on me started."

Noah's forehead crinkled as though he were thinking deeply. He squeezed Lani's shoulder. "We should get going. I have to get back to the office."

Though his touch was intended to be friendly, it still sent a spark of energy through her. Years from now, would she finally be able to be around him without having that kind of response? She had to accept reality. Noah was her boss. Her dream was to be an NYPD K-9 cop. The less she nursed the feelings of attraction, the sooner they would fade. Noah was a handsome man. Sooner or later he'd meet someone and get married. They would both move on with their lives.

Lani and Noah rose to their feet, thanked the doctor and left the office, then got into the elevator.

Noah stared at the elevator doors as they closed. "That was illuminating."

She watched the numbers flash by. "Yes, but it doesn't get us any closer to bringing him in."

Once they were outside, Noah spoke up. "Where did you park? I'll walk you to your car."

After scaring herself over what was probably just in her imagination in the high-rise, Lani was grateful for the escort to her car.

Noah opened the car door for her. "I'm parked in a lot up the street."

She got into her car but left the door open so she could talk to Noah. "Okay, let me know if anything breaks with the Martin Fisher case."

"You got it."

She shut the car door, resting her hands on the steering wheel but not ready yet to pull out. A day off gave her too much time to think about Noah. She did better when she was on duty.

She heard the screech of tires. She couldn't see anything in her rearview mirror. She jumped out of her car and stared down the ramp where a motorcycle was barreling toward Noah as he sprinted to get out of its path.

FOURTEEN

With the motorcycle coming straight for him from behind, Noah ran toward the protection of the parked cars. The roar of the motorcycle engine seemed to surround him. Before he could get to the cars, a blunt object hit him from behind. He fell to the ground and rolled. His vision blurred as he looked up at the taillight of the motorcycle and the man, Martin Fisher, no doubt, holding a crowbar. Pain shot through Noah's back where he'd been hit when he tried to get to his feet.

The motorcycle did a tight turn and headed toward Noah once again. He had an image of the tires running over his back. Again, he tried to get to his feet but the pain was too severe. He crawled toward the safety of the cars, which were still five yards away.

He heard the screech of car tires and the thump of brakes being pushed with force. Lani had pulled up beside him. He reached up for the passenger side door and crawled into the front seat.

Behind Lani's car, Martin swerved around them and then headed up the ramp. Lani hit the gas before Noah had even closed the door. Still dazed, he struggled to click his seat belt into place.

She turned the wheel and her car barely missed the parked vehicles. Martin whizzed by on the down ramp. Though her car was not as nimble as the motorcycle she hurried after him down the ramp and out into the noonday traffic. By the time she got through the exit and out on the street, the motorcycle was not visible.

"Valiant effort. I'll call it into dispatch. Maybe they can catch him." He made the call offering a description of the motorcycle. He spoke into the phone. "Also if they don't catch up with him, put an officer on pulling the footage in the parking garage to see if we can get a plate number."

She slammed her hand on the steering wheel. "This has gone too far. Now he wants to take out the people I care about. The other times he hurt you to get to me."

"Thank you. I care about you too." Noah felt his smile turn to a grimace as pain shot around his torso.

"I'm taking you to the ER," she said.

He wasn't in a place where he could argue. At the very least, he was badly bruised.

Lani drove looking straight ahead. Her jaw had turned to stone.

So this is what she looked like when she was angry. Still as pretty as ever, but the intensity of her rage seemed to suck all the oxygen out of the car.

"Thanks for saving me before I got run over."

"This never should have happened." She spoke through gritted teeth. "We have to do something."

"We're making progress. We have a name to go with the face. He's got to be living somewhere."

Lani didn't respond. She wove in and out of traffic, taking risks that she normally wouldn't take.

"I'd like to get to the ER alive."

She let up on the gas. "Sorry."

She took the exit that led to the hospital, rolling through several streets before pulling into the parking lot by the ER entrance.

He leaned forward to unfasten his seat belt. The radiating pain made him wince, but he didn't make any noise.

Lani unbuckled quickly. "Stay put. Let me get you out."

"I can handle it." Now he was the crabby one. He didn't like needing help. The level to which she was tuned in to his emotions stunned him. He thought he was hiding his pain, but she'd picked up on it.

By the time Lani got around to his side of the car, he'd opened the door and swung his legs out. He raised a palm to her. "I don't want your help." He braced his hand on the door frame and pulled himself up. His lips were pressed together and the pain seemed to be twisting all the way around his rib cage, but he got to his feet.

"You don't need to be a superhero. He hit you pretty hard." He thought he saw just a touch of amusement cross her face.

Grateful for the change of mood he smiled as well. "Sorry, I have to act like such a tough guy." Time to swallow some of that Jameson pride.

"This has upset both of us." She held out an elbow so he could grab her arm for support, which he took. Once they were inside, Noah was taken in for an exam that revealed cuts on his hands and knees and bruised ribs. The X-ray of his back didn't show any damage to vital organs though he had a feeling he was going to be sore for a few days.

The doctor, a man who didn't look like he was more

than twenty, came in after the nurse had wrapped his ribs. "You are free to go. You need to rest for a few days at least and I've written you a prescription for painkillers."

Noah slipped off the exam table and grabbed his shirt. He shook the doctor's hand. "Thanks. I sit at a desk most of the day, so I should be okay."

"Actually, I'd take a couple of days off and really rest," said the doctor.

Noah felt like the doctor was speaking in a foreign language. Jamesons worked, that's who they were. A couple of days off would drive him up the wall. He'd seen how Carter had struggled after being shot. Doing nothing was not in the Jamesons' vocabulary.

"At least take your work home with you and sit in an easy chair," said the doctor.

Noah picked up his paperwork and found Lani sitting in the waiting room. She rose to her feet when she saw him. Something in her expression was different. She wasn't angry anymore, there was a look of resolve in those blue eyes.

"What did the doctor say?"

"Rest…tall order for me."

"Noah, I've been thinking. What if we lure Martin out by setting a trap for him using me as bait," she said.

The words seemed to echo through Noah's brain. He couldn't risk Lani being hurt or worse.

"We know he watches me enough that he's figured out my schedule and routines. He's not working, so he has all kinds of time on his hands. If there was some way to provoke him to come out into the open, to come after me while I was wearing a wire and a team was set up. We might be able to get him to confess to Jordan's murder. We can definitely file charges for his attacks on me."

Noah wasn't sold on the idea, but maybe there was a way to make it work that ensured Lani's safety. "We know he's provoked when he thinks you and I are an item. Maybe we can get him to come after me again and this time I'll be ready for him."

"But you're in no kind of shape to get into a fight," Lani said. "I'm assuming he waits for me to leave my house in the morning or he hangs in the shadows around headquarters then follows me."

"This is going to take a while to plan and set up. I should be feeling better in a week or so. But yes—you and I should make it look like we're seriously dating since he thinks I'm your boyfriend."

Lani blinked as though the remark had hurt her. "What do you mean exactly?"

"I'll pick you up. We'll go out someplace in public where if he's following you, he'll see us. He's watching from a distance. He's never getting close enough to hear our conversation and know that we're not involved. You're right, he probably does have a way to watch you leave your house."

"What's to stop him from going after either one of us before we're ready?" she said.

"He's never attacked with people around. He only taunted you at the parade. I'm sure I can talk Zach and maybe another officer into standing by in case something does go down."

"Reed would lend a hand too." She was silent for a moment. "So we stay in public places until he's good and angry. Then maybe I can go for a bike ride or a jog.

I'll wear a wire and go to an area where there aren't many people but the team can be in place watching."

Noah knew Lani well enough not to argue with her now, but he hoped it didn't come to her being the bait. Next time Martin came after him, Noah intended to be ready.

Before she entered the living room, Lani took one more glance at herself in her full-length mirror. She had gone to way too much trouble for her pretend date with Noah. The pastel purple dress and sapphire necklace brought out the blue in her eyes. She'd braided her blond hair into a French braid.

Reed, Abigail and Dominic were in the living room playing a board game.

Reed smiled at her. "You look great."

"Like a princess ready for the ball," said Abigail.

"Hardly," said Lani. "Just another day on the job."

"Are you sure they have enough officers covering you?" Reed asked, concern etched on his face.

"Noah knows what he is doing." Reed had so little free time to spend with Abigail, she didn't like making him feel like he had to give up even more of it for her. "Enjoy your night off."

The doorbell rang. Lani walked over and opened it. Noah stood dressed in tan pants and a button-down shirt.

They got into his car and he pulled out onto the street.

"I picked a restaurant that has outdoor seating. Zach and Tony are already in place. One at the bistro and one across the street."

"Sounds like you have everything set up." Almost

like a real date. She had to admit to the sadness she felt over it not being real.

"Both Zach and Tony have a photograph of Martin. Chances are, he'll stay out of sight but if they see him, we can grab him. And this will all be over."

Both of them kept checking traffic through the windows and the mirrors. There was no sign of the motorcycle or the dark sedan. Though Martin was clearly unstable, he wasn't stupid. He may have rented or borrowed a car.

Once they were at the bistro, Noah requested a table close to the sidewalk. Lani spotted Tony Knight immediately. He was at the bar sipping a soda. A baseball hat covered his brown hair. Lani didn't know that much about Tony. She hadn't worked with him much. She did know that he'd been Jordan's best friend.

It wasn't until they had ordered that she noticed Zach on the other side of the street standing at the window of a bookstore that stayed open late. A moment before, Zach had been seated at a table inside the bookstore, his face hidden behind a magazine.

Lani glanced around not seeing anyone with Martin's build. He could be peering at them through any one of the windows of the high-rise across the street.

"We should make it look like you and I are really enjoying each other's company," said Noah.

"Who would have thought my acting skills would come in handy?" The only problem was, she wasn't acting. She leaned her head closer to him, resting her chin in her palm and gazing into his eyes. "How's this?" That spark of attraction caused a flare in Noah's eyes. She wasn't imagining things, he must feel it too. She pushed aside the intense feelings and opted for humor. "See, I'm acting like I'm hanging on your every word."

"If only." Noah snorted a laugh, which made her laugh too.

He bent his head as well and continued to laugh. They talked through the meal and a cup of tea. Lani loved hearing the stories of the pranks the Jamesons had pulled on each other as kids.

Once the meal was over, Lani rose to her feet. Zach had repositioned himself on the same side of the street as the bistro. He stood beside a food cart holding a hot dog. Tony still sat at the bar.

When she turned to step out to the sidewalk, Noah put his hand on her back and leaned close to her. Anyone watching would think they were on a date.

Noah glanced at the windows of the high-rise and then up the busy street. She turned to face him. He leaned in and kissed her on the cheek. The kiss, though brief, melted her feet in her shoes. His hand lingered on her neck.

"So it looks like a real date?" Her voice held a note of bitterness. "That's what the kiss was about, right?"

He nodded, and she thought her heart would break. It was all just part of the job. And Martin hadn't even made an appearance. They both got into the car. No one could see them in here.

Noah stared at the steering wheel. "Lani?"

"Yes?"

He turned to face her, his eyes filled with warmth. He leaned closer to her. His Adam's apple moved up and down.

Feeling the pull of his gaze, she leaned toward him.

He covered her mouth with his. His hand rested on her neck and she scooted even closer to him.

He pulled his hand away from her neck. "You deserve a real kiss, not something for show." He lowered his head. "Sorry if I crossed a boundary." His forehead creased, and he leaned toward her, his eyes searching. "Lani, I care about you so much. This is such an impossible situation. The unit needs me as chief."

"I know." She nodded even as the tears warmed her eyes. She was still light-headed from the power of his kiss. She touched her palm to her chest. Her heart was racing. "I suppose we did cross a line. But I don't regret it." She was glad she knew what a real kiss from Noah was like. Even if it could only be this one time.

Noah put the key in the ignition as a faint smile graced his face. "Yeah, me either. But now we have to go back to being just friends."

Her stomach twisted into a knot. "Agreed."

While Noah healed from his injuries, they spent more time together out in the open at the park and in other high-profile public places with no sign of Martin for days. He sent her no texts or notes. She was beginning to wonder if maybe after injuring Noah, Martin had skipped town. Somehow, she didn't think he would give up his obsession that easily.

Once Noah was back to a hundred percent and authorization had been given to put a team in place, they made plans for Lani to ride her bike to a remote part of Flushing Meadows Corona Park. The decision was made to set things up in early evening when there would be fewer people in the park and Lani would look more vulnerable.

The team, which consisted of Reed, Noah, Tony and Lani, met in Noah's office where Lani was fitted with a wire. Noah brought up a map of the park and pointed out each man's position in relationship to where Lani would fake an injury on her bike.

Noah pointed to the spots on the map. "I'll have visual on her up here from this gazebo. Tony and Reed, you'll be able to hear her. If we need to shift positions, I will radio you. Wait for my signal before we move in."

Reed gave Lani a hug before he and Tony took off to drive to the park and get in position. So there was no chance of Martin knowing what was going on, Lani and Noah would leave in separate vehicles.

Once Tony and Reed were gone, Noah closed out the program that had the map of the park. "Give us a half hour before you take off."

"Okay."

"I'm not wild about this plan," he said. "I'm concerned about the level of danger it puts you in. You're still new to being an officer."

"Noah, I want this to be over with. If this doesn't draw him out, nothing will." A knot of tension formed at the base of Lani's neck. Her chest felt tight. She'd be lying to herself if she said she wasn't afraid. "I could use a hug."

He gathered her into his arms. She relished the warmth and safety of his embrace. They lingered for a long moment before he pulled back and gave her a smile that warmed her to the marrow. She'd settle for being Noah's friend if that was all he could offer.

Scotty let out a little protest groan from the corner of the room where he rested on his bed.

Noah laughed. "He hates it when he's not part of the

hug." Noah kneeled. "Come here, boy." Scotty trotted over to him and Noah rubbed his ears.

Lani kneeled as well. "Who's a good boy?" Scotty licked her face.

Noah locked her in his gaze. "Take him with you... for my piece of mind. Scotty will protect you until I can get there."

Lani continued to stroke Scotty's square head. She petted his back and he leaned against her. "Okay."

Noah opened a drawer and pulled out his shoulder holster with his handgun. He slipped into a jacket. He squeezed her shoulder. "Let's do this." He stepped out of the office. She stood at the door and watched him walk past Sophie's desk and then disappear down a hallway.

Lani turned her attention back to Scotty. "Okay, I guess it's just you and me." Lani left headquarters with Scotty. Her mountain bike was already loaded on top of her car. She drove out to the park. At one point while she switched lanes, she thought she caught a glimpse of a motorcycle several lanes over before a car blocked her view.

A van without windows was parked on the far end of the lot. The techs were in there listening to all the communication. The other three officers had probably parked in a different lot. Another car with a bike on top of it pulled into the lot. She didn't have a clear view of the driver. Her heart pounded all the same.

Lani turned her head sideways speaking into her shoulder where the microphone had been placed. "I'm in place. ETA to the spot on the trail is about ten minutes." She unloaded her bike. Earlier in the day, she had parked where her car could be seen from the street so that if Martin was watching her, he would know she had plans to go for a bike ride. The trail she would be going on was one she frequented.

Scotty would run beside. If he was in the habit of doing that with Noah, he'd probably get the idea.

She stared out at the Unisphere, a giant metal globe which was the central feature of the park, visible from almost anywhere. The park had a museum, zoo and amusement rides for kids, but she would be avoiding those for a quieter spot. Flushing Meadows Corona Park was big, the second largest after Central Park, providing lots of places for Martin to make his move.

Her heart was pounding from a mixture of excitement and fear by the time she got on her bike and headed toward the trail. She called over her shoulder. "Come on, Scotty." Scotty ran after her while still on the leash.

In fading light of day, she encountered only a few other bicyclists and walkers. When she looked over her shoulder, Scotty was bounding behind her. She pedaled, watching the trail up ahead. Other side trails intersected with this one. She came to a crossroads, still seeing no other bicyclists in either direction. When she slowed, she could hear Scotty panting.

She arrived at the spot where she was to wait to see if Martin showed up. She lay down her bike, gave a little yell as though she were injured and sat down. Scotty came up beside her.

She listened to the rustling of the fall leaves. A gust of wind pulled some from the trees and sent them swirling through the air. Her heart pounded in her chest.

She tuned her ears hoping to hear the whirring of bike pedals or the pounding of feet on the trail. She knew that Reed was about fifty yards down the hill and Tony was positioned even closer on the other side in a large grove of trees. Up the hill, the gazebo where Noah waited hidden from view was barely visible through the rust- and red-colored bushes.

Pounding footsteps caused her to turn her head back around. In the twilight, she saw a female jogger with reflective gear on coming toward her.

When the woman got close to Lani, she stopped, still jogging in place. "You okay?" She was out of breath.

"Yes, just resting," said Lani.

The woman nodded and disappeared down a side trail. Her footsteps fading into silence.

Scotty hunkered over to her and sat down beside her, pressing his solid muscular body against her side.

Lani turned her attention back to her surroundings. She glanced back up to the gazebo. Her breath caught in her throat. A shadowy figure was moving toward Noah's hiding place.

FIFTEEN

Noah peered through the lattice of the gazebo using small binoculars. He could see Lani's bright purple workout suit as well as the reflective gear she wore on her feet and headband. Scotty's reflective collar was visible as well in the gray light of evening.

He let out a heavy breath. So far nothing.

His chest squeezed tight over the anxiety he battled about putting Lani in this kind of danger. He understood her frustration and that she wanted to get on with her life and her training as a K-9 cop. Rookies always felt like they needed to prove themselves. That had to be part of it.

He could see her blond ponytail bobbing as she petted Scotty who had come to sit beside her. He cared about her so much and wanted more than a friendship with her. He knew it would be out of place for him to ask her to transfer to a different unit in the NYPD. She had her heart set on being a K-9 cop.

He heard a scuffle behind him. Noah turned just as a huge muscular body came down on him like a ton of bricks. Martin Fisher had found him. Though he was caught off guard, and he was in a kneeling position,

Noah managed to angle slightly away so he didn't take the full impact of Martin falling on him.

Tech support and the other men couldn't hear the sound of the fight unless he radioed them. Only Lani was wired.

Martin placed all his weight on Noah's shoulder, pinning him in place. He raised a fist to deliver a blow to Noah's neck.

Noah gasped for air from the impact.

Martin grabbed Noah's hair on the crown of his head and pressed his face close to Noah's.

"You stay away from her. She's mine."

Even in the dim light, Noah could make out the arched eyebrows and gaunt features. Martin's eyes held the glazed quality of a man who was living in his own world.

Even as he fought for breath, he raised his free hand and managed to get a punch into Martin's side and then his stomach.

The man groaned from the pain of impact but remained in place. Martin's strength was stunning. Martin landed more blows to Noah's face and then to his solar plexus.

Again, Noah fought for breath.

He used his knee to pummel Martin's back. The move seemed to take Martin by surprise. The weight on Noah's shoulder lessoned.

Noah struggled to twist free.

Martin hit him again. This time in the head. The blows left Noah dazed.

Martin shifted so both of his knees shoved into Noah's stomach. Reaching for his gun was not possible.

Martin pulled a needle from his back pocket. Uncapped it and held it up.

Noah fought harder to break free using his knees again to throw Martin off kilter before he could stick the needle in Noah. Jordan had died from a drug injection. More evidence that Noah was in a fight with Jordan's killer.

The distant bark of a dog, of his dog, reached the gazebo. The barking grew louder and more intense. Lani must have seen Martin enter the gazebo and was headed up the hill with Scotty.

Martin's eyes grew round. He looked one way and then the other.

"Lani and the dog are on their way," said Noah.

"She's got quite a hike up the hill," said Martin. The inflection in his words gave away that he was afraid.

He grabbed Noah's radio off his shoulder and tore it free. Noah reached for Martin's shirt collar and yanked hard enough to put Martin off balance. Martin clawed at Noah's face and then slammed his fist back into Noah's chest. Noah released his grip on Martin as he wheezed in air. He felt like he was breathing through a straw.

Martin hit Noah a couple more times. Noah feared he would pass out. Fueled by mental instability, Martin's strength was almost superhuman.

In the seconds when Noah was trying to orient himself and regain focus, Martin bolted from the gazebo.

Still dizzy, Noah leaped to his feet and took off after Martin, who disappeared into some brush. He must have dropped the needle somewhere. It would be too dangerous to hold on to an uncapped needle. He glanced around as he hurried after Martin. Finding the needle would be close to impossible. Now he wished Scotty was with him. The dog would have no trouble tracking Martin.

Noah ran after him, still not at full strength. Keeping his eyes on the shaking branches that indicated which direction Martin had gone, Noah willed himself to move faster.

He took in as deep a breath as he dared. His ribs still hurt from his injury.

Noah saw a flash of color. Martin had veered off the path into the thick of the trees. There was still enough brush and foliage on the trees to conceal him.

Aware that he risked hitting an innocent bystander if he wasn't careful, Noah pulled his gun.

Scotty's bark persisted, dying off now and then when he must have been sniffing the ground. A fearful person on the run emitted a scent that was easy for dogs to track. Noah dashed into the trees, he turned one way and then another, studying the landscape for any sign of movement. He had to assume that Reed and Tony would move in as well. Lani could communicate with them.

A squirrel ran up a thick oak tree and he could hear the traffic on the expressway far in the distance. He turned in a half circle, still looking. Martin was dressed in neutral colors, tan and browns, that would make it hard to spot him. He saw a jogger in bright colors on another path.

Noah stepped deeper into the trees. Though he could not say why, his cop instinct told him that Martin was close. He could feel the weight of a gaze on him. The brush got thicker and more overgrown as he got farther from the trail. His pulse drummed in his ears. He pushed a tree branch out of the way. He had to bend his knees and almost crawl to get through.

Somewhere off to the side a tree branch broke. A woman on a bicycle dressed in neon colors whizzed by on a parallel trail.

A weight landed on Noah's back and pushed down on his shoulders. Noah fell forward when Martin jumped him from behind. He fell on a bush that collapsed beneath him. Branches scratched his face.

Martin wrapped his hands around Noah's neck. The move meant Noah's arms and legs were still free. Martin's he-man grip around Noah's neck had the potential to be lethal. Noah's vision filled with black dots as he tried to twist free. Firing his gun would put innocent people at too great a risk.

He needed to break free before he lost consciousness or couldn't breathe anymore. He could feel Martin's breath on his ear as he stood behind Noah and suctioned even tighter around Noah's neck. Noah jabbed an elbow into Martin's stomach.

The blow didn't even seem to faze Martin. He continued to cut off Noah's air. Noah knew the lightheadedness meant he was about to pass out. He struggled for breath. With the final bit of energy and focus he had left, he jabbed Martin three times with his elbow. Martin let up on Noah's neck and stepped back.

Noah choked and gasped for air even as he lunged at Martin. The attack had left Noah weak.

The sound of Scotty working his way toward them grew even louder. He heard sirens in the distance. Lani must have called in reinforcements. Tony and Reed must be moving in as well. Martin's eyes grew round with fear, and he dashed into the underbrush.

Still unfocused and stumbling around from nearly being choked to death, Noah spotted the purple of Lani's outfit moving through the trees. Scotty ran up ahead of her. Reed and Tony were close behind her.

"Boy am I glad to see you. He went off this way."

Scotty had already picked up the scent and was pushing through the underbrush like a four-legged bulldozer. They raced after Scotty as he led them toward a trail. Scotty bolted along with Lani and Noah at his heels. The dog stopped, sniffed the ground and then left the trail. Noah couldn't see Martin anywhere, but he trusted Scotty's nose.

The sirens grew louder. No doubt, officers would be in all the parking lots that surrounded the park. When he glanced through the trees, he saw Reed and Tony searching as well. Martin wasn't going to get away this time.

Lani spoke into her hidden radio. "I think we're in the northeast corner of the park. I'm with Noah."

They continued to work their way through the trees. Scotty lost the scent when they came to an open area where there were several sleeping bags stuffed in the brush and evidence that a fire had been built.

They came toward a busier part of the park where parents watched their children on the carousel. Martin could easily fade into the crowd.

Scotty continued to sniff the ground. All the human smells were making it hard for him to find Martin's scent.

"Let's keep looking. Uniformed officers are going to be in all the parking lots, so he won't go back to his car if he parked in one of them." Noah commanded Scotty to follow him. They searched the area where the crowds were coming to the street that bordered the park.

The sound of New York coming alive at night reached his ears as they came to the edge of the park. A sea of faces. Martin was smart. He'd stop running and blend in with the crowd.

Scotty heeled beside Noah while Lani walked on the other side of him.

They searched up and down several streets before giving up. If Scotty picked up on Martin's scent at all, he would alert. The dog remained close to Noah, sniffing the air and the ground but not giving any sign that Martin might be close. Noah tried to not give in to the sense of defeat that he felt.

They walked for several more blocks before Lani spoke into the radio. "This is Officer Lani Branson and Chief Noah Jameson. Could you come pick us up? We're headed back toward the northwest entrance to the park."

Maybe one of the other officers was able to nab Martin. Maybe Reed or Tony had caught up with him. From the sound of the sirens, NYPD had pulled out all the stops to try to catch the guy. Somehow, though, he doubted they'd gotten him. Martin was slippery. And he and Lani were the ones who had gotten the closest to him. Noah was 90 percent sure Martin had eluded them.

The only thing that was clear to Noah was that as long as Martin was on the streets neither he nor Lani was safe.

As Noah drove Lani back to her house, she could feel a weariness settling into her muscles. Once again,

Martin had escaped them only to fade into the crowd of people. News had come over the radio that a stolen car had been left at one of the parking lots surrounding the park. Martin had probably arrived in that.

Noah had not spoken much since he had offered to take her home. She didn't feel too talkative herself. Now it felt like this thing with Martin would go on forever. Would she be free of him if she moved out of the city? The thought caused her pain; she'd have to leave everything she cared about. Her job, her brother, her home and Noah.

From the backseat, Scotty nudged against her cheek and groaned. The dog was amazing in how he picked up on her mood. She stroked Scotty's square jaw. The thought of not being a K-9 officer would break her heart. The truth was she felt like she was in her element when she worked with the dogs.

Noah cleared his throat. "So you texted Reed?"

"Yes, he just made it home." Noah and Lani had hung around the park to see if there was any sign of Martin and to wait until the vehicle that probably belonged to Martin had been located, which ended up taking a couple of hours. The forensic team was still going over it.

Not catching Martin had triggered a restlessness in Lani. She couldn't stay in limbo for much longer. Something needed to change in her professional and personal life. Reed and Abigail were talking more about wedding plans and finalizing adopting Dominic. Maybe she could look into being a K-9 officer in another borough. Maybe then her intense feelings for Noah would fade. She turned her attention to him.

"Martin attacked you too," she said. "He might do it again."

"I'll be all right," Noah said. "I live in a house with a bunch of Jameson men."

Lani suspected Noah was saying that to keep her from worrying. His father was still in good shape but older. Carter was injured and Zach no longer lived in the house since he'd gotten married.

"I suppose you've got Scotty to protect you, and the other dogs," she said.

"Don't worry about me, Lani." Noah drove a few more blocks before speaking up. "This will go in my report tomorrow, but when Martin attacked me he had a needle with him. Jordan was killed by drug overdose administered with a needle, remember? We have Forensics working with the dogs to find the needle."

"Criminals usually use the same methods most of the time. That certainly makes it more likely that Martin did kill Jordan."

"We don't know anything yet for sure. We need evidence. Katie sometimes comes into headquarters to have lunch with Sophie. If you see her, please don't say anything."

Noah double-parked in front of the house where the glow from the lights in the living room and kitchen indicated that Reed was home.

Noah leaned toward her. "Don't worry about me."

Though she didn't feel it on the inside, she gave Noah a faint smile and reassurance. "You have a good rest of your night, Noah."

Lani hurried up the sidewalk. As she unlocked the door and stepped inside, she heard Noah pulling away from the curb. From the moment she stepped inside her home, something felt wrong. Reed wasn't on the couch or in the kitchen.

"Reed?" No answer.

From inside the garage, Jessie's muffled baying reached Lani's ears. Reed never left the bloodhound in the garage. It was reserved for the upstairs tenant. Lani hurried to her bedroom to grab her gun, pulling her phone out so she could call Noah. He couldn't be more than a few blocks away.

The lights in the house went out. Someone had thrown a breaker. She fumbled with her phone to click on the flashlight. She didn't hear the upstairs tenant walking around. He must be out.

Hands grabbed her from behind jerking her back. She dropped her phone. Before he even spoke, she knew it was Martin.

"You're coming with me. You were meant to be with me."

Lani struggled to twist away. She kicked Martin in the shin, one of the vulnerable parts on the human body. Martin didn't so much as groan in pain. His grip remained locked tight on her. She couldn't get the leverage to try for Martin's knees or his stomach. The other vulnerable parts of the body.

He dragged her across the floor, swinging her around to face the garage door where Jessie was still putting up a fuss. Certainly, the neighbors would begin to wonder what all the noise was about.

"Now open the door," said Martin.

He released her from his grasp. She felt something hard and solid press against her back, a gun.

"Where is Reed?" Her voice trembled. Had Martin killed her brother in order to get to her?

"Open the door," Martin said, his voice filled with rage.

She twisted the knob. Jessie whined when she saw Lani and lunged toward her. The dog was tied up in a corner on a short rope unable to move more than a few feet.

"Doesn't that dog ever shut up? Thought if I put her out here she'd be quiet."

"Not when she's distressed." Lani looked around the garage for something to fight Martin with. The tenant's tools were on the far wall.

Exhausted, Jessie lay down but continued to whine.

"Now go to the outside door and open it." Martin shoved the gun in her back as a reminder of who was in control.

She swung open the door. Martin had parked his car in a side street where no one would see it.

"Put your hands behind you."

Lani hesitated, trying to figure out a way to get the gun from Martin.

"Do it now!" Martin's voice filled with rage.

Reluctantly, she did as she was told even as she looked around for an escape route. The next-door neighbor had a high fence in his backyard. No one would be out at this hour anyway.

Martin secured her hands.

She felt a pinprick in her left shoulder and then the sense that some venomous substance was moving through her veins.

"Just to make sure you don't try to get away." Martin opened the back car door and shoved her in.

Lani had a fearful moment of wondering if whatever Martin had given her was going to kill her. As they rolled through the streets, she realized it was probably just meant to weaken her so she wouldn't fight back. She remained conscious, but it would take all her strength to even sit up in the car, let alone find a way to escape.

She was trapped in a car with a volatile man who had probably already murdered once before.

SIXTEEN

The phone call awoke Noah from a deep sleep. It was his brother Zach. Noah still felt groggy. "Yes?"

"Reed just phoned in. Martin came to their house and disabled Reed so he could kidnap Lani. Reed got away and was able to get the license plate number of the sedan as he chased Martin down. Reed lost him, but Patrol spotted the sedan at the marina. We think he has her on the boat."

Noah's head felt like it might explode from the news Zach delivered. His stomach turned to a hard rock. He was still trying to wake up, still trying to process what Zach was telling him.

He threw back the covers, swung his legs to the floor and bolted to his feet in one swift motion. "Get the coast guard involved. I'm going to commission a chopper. We need to find that boat."

"Ten-four."

"Keep me posted," said Noah. "Tracking dogs and search and rescue on standby. I'm taking Scotty with me."

As he dressed, his heart squeezed tight. He bent over from the fear that washed through him. Lani was in

Martin's clutches. There was no telling what Martin might do. He straightened and took in a breath. He had to stay strong for Lani.

He headed toward the door. "Come on, Scotty, we got work to do."

Scotty trailed behind him.

Within half an hour, he was at the police helipad. Reed met him there with a scarf that had belonged to Lani. It had her scent on it in case they had to track her that way.

With the blade whirring, creating a tremendous wind, he loaded Scotty into the backseat, and he got in the front with the pilot. He put his headset on. His stomach lurched as they rose into the air. He'd been in a chopper dozens of times. The tightening in his stomach was about Lani. His world would fall apart if something happened to her.

When Noah glanced over his shoulder, Scotty sat firmly in the seat, his head held high and alert. Something about seeing his partner ready to work and face whatever lay ahead gave him strength.

News came from the coast guard that they thought they had spotted the boat headed toward the East River but the boat had evaded them. The helicopter pilot headed in that direction. Noah stared down below to search the water. There were no flashing lights indicating a boat down there. Maybe Martin had turned off the lights on the boat to avoid detection.

Noah commanded the chopper to fly lower. His eyes searched everywhere. For Lani's sake, he would not let his fear overtake him. He needed to remain cool and focused if he was to find her and save her from Martin.

He thought he saw shadows that looked different from the rest of the water.

He gave the pilot the signal to lose elevation.

"Any lower and I'm going to end up in the water." The pilot spoke through his headset. "Night vision goggles in that compartment by your seat."

Noah put on the goggles and continued to survey the water. He leaned out of the chopper even more. Then he saw it. It was not that an outline of the boat came into view, but he saw the effects of a boat on the water, the triangular shaped ridges created in the wake of a boat pushing through the current.

"Can you angle off toward there and shine the light?" he spoke to the pilot.

"Gonna have to get a little elevation first," said the pilot.

It took a few minutes for the chopper to get higher and then switch on the light. It was a boat all right, headed toward North Brother Island, an abandoned island between the Bronx and Rikers Island.

"Back off. I don't want him to know we're using the chopper to search for him. Make it look like we're moving away from him." If Martin figured out he'd been seen, it could endanger Lani even more. "You've got to put me down on the other side of North Brother where he's not likely to see or hear that we landed there."

"That's a tall order," said the pilot. "I'll do my best."

The pilot gained elevation and angled away, making it look like they were headed toward the Bronx. Martin would just think the chopper was on a regular patrol or was a private hire for a tourist. It looked like Martin was taking the boat to dock on the north side of the island. The pilot came in low on the west side. There were numerous buildings that would block the view of his landing. The buildings, most of them brick, were crumbling and overgrown with plant life.

Before the turn of the last century, the island had housed people with infectious diseases. After that it had been a home for veterans and heroin addicts. But no one had been on the island since the early 1960s and it was illegal to go there. It was a perfect hiding place for someone like Martin.

The pilot brought them down in an open area and killed the motor.

"Wait here for me," said Noah to the pilot as he jumped out and commanded Scotty to get out as well. Once the noise of the chopper died down, Noah phoned Zach and let him know where he was. Zach promised that backup was on the way. It would take them a while to get there.

Noah pulled the scarf Reed had given him out of his jacket. He held it to his own nose, drinking in the light floral scent of Lani's perfume. His heart filled with longing. He had to find her. He put the scarf away.

They would need to get over to the other side of the island where Martin had docked before Scotty could pick up a scent. He pulled his flashlight out. Once he got close to where Martin had Lani, he'd have to navigate in the darkness. He tugged on Scotty's leash.

"Let's go find her."

The dog took off running. Noah kept up with the steady pace that Scotty set.

Martin finally kidnapping Lani instead of just tormenting her probably indicated that something inside of his obsessed brain had snapped.

Yes, backup was on its way, but Noah knew that right

now Lani's life hung in the balance. It was up to him and his K-9 partner to bring her home safe.

Lani could feel the waves hitting the boat as it chugged through the water and finally came to a stop. She'd been in such a weakened state from the drugs that Martin had had no trouble lifting her onto the boat from the car. Only now as the boat was docking did she feel the drugs wearing off and her strength returning. She had no idea where he'd taken her. Lying on her stomach with her hands tied behind her had not given her much of a view of her surroundings.

Martin pressed his foot on her calf. "Don't try anything. I need to tie the boat off."

She heard his feet pound across the deck and then onto the pier.

She attempted to roll over and to sit up. Even that took substantial effort. All she could see were shadows on the landscape and stars twinkling overhead.

Martin climbed back on the boat. He crossed his arms and stared at her. "Well don't you look pretty in the moonlight. My beautiful Katie girl." His voice held a slimy quality.

His words sent a new wave of fear through her. So in his twisted mind, Martin had become convinced that she was Katie. If she broke the news to him that she wasn't Katie, what would the effect be? Would it put him over the edge? She knew he was capable of violence. Or was the lie so entrenched in his mind that reality could not get in?

He stomped over to her. "Let me help you to your feet, my dear." He cupped her elbow.

The boat rocked in the water as she stared around at

what looked like an end-of-the-world scene. Buildings crumbling and leaning to one side, piles of rubble everywhere, the plant life was consuming what men had built. This had to be North Brother Island. She'd seen pictures but never been here. Though it was illegal to step onto the island, urban adventurers and teenagers on a dare still came here from time to time.

"Why have you brought me here?"

"It's my hiding place, my sanctuary. We won't be here for long. Just until the heat is off of us. Then I'll take you to someplace nice for our honeymoon." He tugged on her elbow. "Come, I'll show you."

He led her to the edge of the boat. Lani steeled herself against the encroaching panic. It did not appear that he intended to harm her...at least not for now.

He climbed over the railing of the boat. "I'm going to have to lift you out."

"I think I can crawl over." She still felt weak from having been drugged. It would be a balancing act with her hands tied behind her back, but the thought of Martin touching her sent chills all over her skin.

"I said, let me lift you." A note of rage had entered his voice.

So that's what it took. If she was at all disagreeable, if she didn't do exactly as he requested, he might turn on her. Was he capable of murder? If he *was* Jordan Jameson's killer, then the answer was yes. She had to assume so.

"Okay, Martin, have it your way."

He wrapped his strong arms around her middle and lifted her like she was made of paper. Again, she was reminded of how she was no match for him physically. Her best hope was to try to outwit him. Maybe if she played along with his bizarre fantasy, his defenses would go down.

He sat her on the dilapidated pier which squeaked from the weight of two people. Some of the wooden floorboards were missing, offering a view of the dark water flowing below.

Again, he cupped her elbow with his hand. "Follow me." He pulled a flashlight out of his pocket and turned it on.

Even if she could get away from him and back to the boat, she'd never operated a boat before. Though she'd watched other people. He led her past a brick building of Victorian design. They stepped through the thick brush and overgrown plant life.

They walked past theater chairs that looked like they were set up for an outdoor program though the chairs were more moss than wood. They entered another brick building. Holes in the roof allowed some moonlight to illuminate the area. Part of the wall had crumbled. She could see an iron bed frame leaning to one side due to a broken leg, and a sink and tub in the far corner.

"This way," said Martin.

Beside a spiral staircase, Martin had made a sort of camp. He had a propane stove, two cots with sleeping bags on them, a supply of canned goods and some other personal items. He gestured toward one of the beds. "Have a seat?"

When she sat down, one of the items on the bed looked like a photo album.

"I'm going to build us a fire to keep us warm," said Martin. He rubbed his hands together.

"Could you untie me, please, Martin?" She tried to sound sweet instead of demanding.

Martin didn't answer right away. He turned and stared at her. It was too dark to read the minute details of his expression. His body language suggested he was relaxed.

"I suppose it wouldn't hurt. Tonight is a special night." He pulled a knife from his shirt pocket. She shifted so her bound hands were toward him. He sawed away at the rope. "You have to promise me, you'll sit still."

"I promise." She sounded sugary sweet. Who would have thought her acting skills would come in handy yet again?

She saw then that he had placed some rocks in a circle and had a supply of wood already stacked and ready to go. While Martin's back was to her as he built the fire, she flipped open the photo album.

Shock spread through her as she turned the pages. Martin had clipped the news stories of Jordan's death. There were photos of Katie at the funeral and standing in the driveway of the Rego Park house. All taken from a distance. There were also drawings of Katie and a poem written to her.

Lani remembered what the psychologist had said about obsession being a twisted, unpredictable condition. The object of desire can just as quickly become the object of hate.

As he built the fire, Martin's shirt rode up to reveal he had shoved the gun in the waistband of his jeans.

She closed the photo album softly, debating if she should try to grab the gun while he was distracted with building the fire. If she failed, he might become violent. Rage would only make him stronger.

Once the fire was going, he turned to face her. "Why

don't you rustle up something for us to eat." The shadow of flames from the fire danced across his face and in his dull, dead eyes.

"Sure, Martin, I can do that." Every muscle in her body felt tight as she rose to her feet and stepped over to where the cookstove had been set on a makeshift table fashioned from bricks and a board.

Somewhere in the distance a bird made a sound that resembled a scream. The brutality of the noise startled her. She remembered reading that North Brother Island was a bird sanctuary.

Her heart pounded as she grabbed a can of beans and the can opener. She lit the stove, raising her gaze slightly to assess her surroundings. Her only hope would be to get to that boat. If she could disable or restrain Martin, she had some chance of figuring out how to operate it and escaping. The only way she could make that happen would be to surprise Martin, and she needed some kind of weapon. He was stronger than her, but she was quicker and understood how to use his strength against him because of her training.

"I know what you are thinking about." His voice pelted her back like tight, hard balls of hail.

She turned slowly to face him.

He held the gun on her. His lip curled up at one end of his mouth.

She swallowed to get rid of the lump in her throat. "I was only thinking about you, Martin." Not a total lie. He continued to stare at her in a way that unnerved her. She had to find a way to reassure him, so he would relax and let his defenses down. If his paranoia went into overdrive, there was no telling what he would do. "I'm just going to cook us a nice meal here and we can enjoy it…together."

He let the gun fall by his side. Her little act of compliance had relaxed him.

She turned her back, put the pan on the stove and stirred the beans. Her stomach was in a tight knot, but her voice had given nothing away.

As she stirred, watching the beans bubble from the heat, she wondered what had happened to her brother. Was Reed alive? Her heart squeezed tight with angst. She massaged her sternum, trying to take in a deep breath. She couldn't get distracted by such dark thoughts. She needed to stay in the moment. No one was coming for her. If she was to escape, it was up to her.

She wondered too if she could get Martin to talk, would he confess to killing Jordan? That was dicey territory. She knew from having witnessed police interrogations that with a stable person, the desire to confess was almost overwhelming. But with Martin, it was hard to know what his response would be. Martin might want to brag about what he'd done…if he had killed Jordan. Or making him face reality might send him over the edge.

She prayed for guidance.

God, show me how to get away.

SEVENTEEN

Noah and Scotty moved silently through the thick underbrush. He'd commanded Scotty not to bark. Though the barking often intimidated and paralyzed a criminal on the run, Noah thought the better strategy would be to surprise Martin.

He heard the lapping of the water before he saw the shoreline and Martin's boat.

Noah could see Martin's boat bobbing at the dock. He hurried over to it where Scotty picked up a scent right away, jerking on the leash.

From the pace that Scotty was setting with his nose close to the ground, Noah knew the scent was hot.

They hurried past dark buildings overtaken by plant life, past piles of bricks and through thick brush.

Scotty stopped abruptly and sat back on his haunches, a hard alert. Noah kneeled beside Scotty, stroking his head and his back. Noah didn't see anything, but if Scotty said they were close, he'd trust his dog's nose over his own senses anytime.

He heard birds feeding in the distance and waves hitting the shore and then…the faint sound of voices.

Crouching, Noah moved in toward the sound. He

signaled for Scotty to follow. The dog trailed behind as they approached, padding softly. Scotty seemed to instinctually know he needed to be quiet.

They pressed against the brick wall. On the other side just feet away, Lani spoke in soothing tones to Martin. Above him was a rectangular opening that must have been a window at one time in the brick building.

"I see that you put together a photo album of Katie." There was a long pause. "You know that I'm not really Katie, right, Martin?"

More silence.

Even though a wall divided them, Noah could sense the tension and hear it in Lani's voice.

Lani prompted. "Martin?"

"Shut up," Martin shouted.

Martin was wound as tight as a coil. Noah could hear pots and pans being banged together. His feet stomped the ground.

Was Lani trying to bring Martin back to a lucid moment with her question?

"What happened to Jordan, Martin?"

He still wasn't sure what she was doing. Was Lani trying to get a confession out of Martin? Or she might be trying to push him over the edge to create an opportunity for escape. If he knew anything, it was that Martin was volatile and unpredictable. All of it was dangerous. Lani still thought she was on her own and had no other choice but to take such a risk.

It was time to move closer and wait for the chance to jump in and extract Lani and, hopefully with Scotty's help, subdue Martin. Noah gave a hand signal for Scotty to follow. He couldn't wait for backup. They circled around the building using the thick brush as cover. Part of the wall where Martin had Lani was deteriorated.

Scotty pressed in close to him as Noah raised his head and assessed the situation.

"You ruined our nice dinner. I know what you are trying to do. You're not going to get away." Martin was in the process of tying up Lani. He bound her wrists in front of her. "I was meant to be with Katie. You're not Katie. I know you're not Katie. Katie is soft and quiet. I don't want anything to do with you. You are a betrayer."

Martin had a gun shoved in the waistband of his belt. A blazing fire crackled. A pan was overturned in the dirt and beans had been spilled.

Once Lani was tied up, Martin paced, rubbing his hands through his hair, his fingers stiff and clawlike.

He continued to pace and get more and more worked up. "You talk. You talk way too much."

Scotty was so close Noah could feel the dog's breath on his cheek. Noah inhaled deeply and pulled his gun. There was never going to be an exact right time. He rose to his feet and aimed his gun knowing that Scotty would jump in at the right moment if needed.

"Put your hands up, Martin."

Both Lani and Martin looked surprised. Martin reached around to his back but then grabbed Lani, yanking her to her feet and holding the gun to her temple.

"Come one step closer and she gets a bullet in her head," said Martin. "I don't care about her anymore. It's Katie I want."

Noah tensed. The last thing he wanted was for Lani to be in danger like this.

"Put the gun down, Martin," said Noah, taking a step toward him, weapon aimed at Martin's chest. Noah didn't want anyone to die here tonight, but sometimes a police officer had no choice. He just wasn't sure if he could pull the shot off without risking Lani's life.

"Come on, Martin, if you kill me—" Lani spoke between jagged breaths "—we can't be together."

Martin jerked Lani around. "I don't want to be with you. I see that now. It's always been Katie. Only Katie."

Noah was afraid Martin's gun would go off accidentally. He was clearly unhinged.

Scotty lunged out of the brush and started barking at Martin. Martin aimed his gun at Scotty.

"No," Lani and Noah shouted at the same time.

Heart racing, Lani slammed against Martin by swinging her bound hands against him. The bullet he'd fired at Scotty went wild.

Noah commanded Scotty to back off.

Martin whirled around and aimed the gun at Lani. "You're coming with me." Then he turned, pointing the gun at the dog and then at Noah. "Try anything and she dies. Put your hands up. Drop your gun."

Scotty growled but stood his ground.

As if to make his point, Martin grabbed Lani by her collar, jerking her back. The cold metal of the gun pressed against her temple. Sweat formed on her forehead, and she took in shallow breaths.

"It's all right, Noah, do what he says." She nodded. Scotty had almost died for her. She couldn't face losing either of them. She'd find a way to get away. And she knew Noah and Scotty wouldn't give up either.

"Drop it now. Toss it toward me," said Martin.

In the seconds that Noah hesitated to respond, she

could tell he was strategizing, trying to figure out the best way to get them out of this situation.

Martin wrapped his free hand around the back of her neck, squeezing tight. He spoke through gritted teeth. "Drop it now."

Noah tossed the gun in Martin's direction. Martin kicked it hard, sending it sailing into the brush. No way would Noah be able to find it quickly.

"If you or that dog comes after me, she is dead, do you hear me?"

Noah nodded. Despite his seeming surrender, Lani knew that he was probably already trying to come up with a plan of attack.

"Now go." Martin pushed on Lani's shoulder to get her to turn and then pressed the gun in her back. Martin craned his neck to check on Noah. "I meant what I said. Try anything and she dies."

Lani dared not turn to see Noah. She'd never been so happy in her life when he and Scotty popped up from behind the rubble. She wasn't in this alone.

"Run," said Martin. "Back to the boat."

Lani took off at a jog slowed by her hands being tied in front of her.

She had every confidence that Noah and Scotty would be after them as soon as Martin couldn't see them anymore. She also sensed that Martin was serious about killing her. Whatever attachment he'd had to her was gone, now that he had experienced the reality of being with her.

Her foot caught on a root and she fell. She twisted to one side to avoid the full impact of falling on her face.

"Get up," said Martin.

"I'd have better balance if you would untie me."

"Quit trying to trick me. I see now you are nothing like my Katie girl." He glanced around nervously and then pointed the gun at her. "I said, get up."

She managed to stand by anchoring her hands in front of her and pushing up with her legs. Still off balance, she swayed when she straightened her torso.

They took off at a steady pace. Once they were free of the tangle of undergrowth and rubble, Lani broke into a jog. She could hear the waves hitting the shore as they drew closer to the boat. Martin's footsteps pounded behind her.

They arrived at the dock.

"Get on the boat." Martin glanced around.

Lani didn't see Noah anywhere but that didn't mean he wasn't right behind them. He and Scotty were probably hidden in the shadows. Once Martin took off in the boat, there was no chance for Noah to get to her. She had to stall for time.

Lani lifted her hands. "I can't step over that rim with my hands tied."

Martin seemed distracted. He stalked toward some trees, aiming his gun at one point and then at another. He turned and stared up the path where they'd just run.

"Martin, you have to cut me loose so I can get into the boat."

He turned back to face her as though seeing her for the first time. He stalked back over to the dock. "I know your game." His wild eyes seemed to burn right through her. Her heart beat faster, and her throat went dry. He lifted her up and put her on the boat as if she was a feather.

She knew in that moment, he would only keep her alive as long as she was of use to him. Holding the gun to her head and threatening to shoot had been enough to make Noah hold back to keep her from being killed. Once Martin was away from the island and there was no danger of being caught, she suspected he'd shoot her and toss her body in the East River.

Frantic, she glanced around again hoping to see some sign that Noah was close.

After unwinding the rope that kept the boat attached to the dock, Martin got onto the boat as well.

She sat on the deck with the autumn breeze making her skin prickle.

Martin got back on the boat and started the engine.

She leaned forward, praying that she would find a way to escape. Praying that Noah would get to her before it was too late.

EIGHTEEN

Noah shivered as he treaded water underneath the dock in the East River. Had he made a mistake to plan his attack this way? He'd gotten to the boat only seconds before he heard Martin coming with Lani through the brush. They had been slowed by Lani being tied up and she had stumbled. There hadn't been time to climb on the boat and hide.

Martin seemed to have a sixth sense about when he was about to be caught. Noah wanted to wait until Martin's defenses were down. There would be no place for Martin to run once the boat was in open water.

He could hear Martin walking around on deck and the boat engine roared to life. As it backed away from the dock, Noah grabbed rope that wrapped around the boat. He'd left Scotty hidden on the shore. He knew he could trust Scotty to stay put until he could come back for him.

The boat putted along. Martin couldn't go very fast in the shallow water.

Behind him, Noah saw a blinking light descending not too far from where Scotty was hiding. He heard the distant whir of a helicopter. Backup was here, but they would not get to the boat fast enough.

Martin cursed at the sight of the helicopter.

The boat picked up speed.

Noah pulled himself up and peered above the rim of the boat. Both Lani and Martin had their backs to him. Lani was tied up. Martin's gun was still in his waistband.

He shivered. The wait in the cold water had left his muscles weakened.

The boat was out in the open now, bumping over the waves. It was now or never. The engine was loud enough that Noah thought he could pull himself in without being heard. He gripped the rim of the boat and hoisted himself on deck. He'd been quiet but Lani must have sensed something, because she turned her head slightly sideways.

Still feeling the effects of having been in the water, Noah got to his feet and bolted the short distance to where Martin stood steering the boat. When he was about two feet away, Martin reached for his gun and turned to face him, raising the gun with his finger on the trigger.

Lani kicked at Martin's legs. He didn't fall down, but the move was enough to set him off balance.

The gun went flying across the deck.

Martin turned his attention back to steering. He drove like a wild man, zigzagging and tilting the boat from side to side. The gun moved back and forth across the deck, and Noah plunged to his knees. Lani slid across the deck as well.

The gun was on the other side of the deck when Martin stopped the boat engine.

Still on his knees, Noah crawled toward the gun. Lani's stalker rushed toward him and kicked him hard in the jaw. Pain radiated through Noah's head and he tasted blood.

The boat continued to sway back and forth. Martin edged toward his weapon.

Noah reached out and grabbed his leg at the ankle and yanked him down. Martin flipped over so he was on his back. He dove toward Noah, who dodged out of the way as Martin, with his almost superhuman strength, came down on him.

Meanwhile, Lani was trying to scoot toward the gun even though her hands were tied.

Noah scrambled to his feet and managed to get a kick into Martin's ribs before the other man could stand up. Once he was on his feet, the terrible unbridled fury that was Martin Fisher dove toward Noah. Noah knew he could not match his strength. He'd have to use his agility and quickness to save himself and Lani.

Noah stepped out of the way. Lani was within inches of being able to pick up the gun. Martin backed him up to the railing of the boat and clutched his neck beneath his chin, squeezing hard and pushing Noah backward.

Noah gasped for air, trying to find a way to break free and keep from being shoved overboard. He let go of the railing with one hand to get in a punch to Martin's stomach, which only caused a minor letup in the pressure on his neck.

Martin released his hold and landed a blow to Noah's stomach and then two to his shoulder in rapid succession. That assault weakened Noah, and Martin pushed him overboard. Noah reached up for the railing as he fell backward.

A gunshot went off on deck. Lani must have recovered the gun. The shot had gone wild. She probably couldn't aim with much accuracy with her hands tied.

"You." Martin stomped across the deck. No doubt to snatch the gun from her.

Noah caught the railing as his feet skimmed the surface of the water. He attempted to pull himself back up on deck. He felt weak from fighting and from having been in the cold water. He managed to get back in the boat flopping like a caught fish.

Martin had yanked the gun from Lani and was aiming it at her. Noah summoned up all the strength he had and charged at Martin's back. This time Martin's stomach pressed against the railing. He heard the gun fall in the water.

Noah had had enough. He was weak and tired, but more than anything, he was tired of Martin tormenting Lani.

He let up pressure on Martin's back. Martin swung around, ready to fight. This time Noah was prepared. His opponent tended to go for the stomach or the head. Noah blocked the punch and landed two to his head, which seemed to stun him.

Martin lunged at Noah, but he dodged out of the way and then brought his clenched fists down on Martin's back. He fell on the deck. Noah landed a final blow to his head, which left him dazed but still conscious.

"That rope over there," said Lani, who was trying to scoot toward some cording.

Noah kept his weight on Martin's back while he struggled to get away and cursed at Noah, but his voice was weak from the struggle and having been hit in the head. Lani dragged the rope across the deck until Noah could reach it. He tied Martin's hands and his feet with the single length of rope. He didn't want any chance of him getting away. After Martin was secure, Noah drew his attention to the island. He saw light everywhere, searchlights and flashlights bobbing. A helicopter hovered over the debris and buildings.

"Why don't I get this boat turned around and we can go get Scotty? Looks like there is plenty of help to deal with Martin," said Noah.

"That sounds like a plan," she said. "Noah, is Reed okay?" Her words were drenched in fear.

"Yes, he's the one who was able to track Martin's car to the dock."

"I was so afraid that…you know."

He could hear the fatigue in her voice as well. He moved across the deck so he could untie her hands. His fingers brushed over her palm as he worked the knots free. He clamped his hand on her shoulder and whispered in her ear. "It's over."

She turned toward him, and he gathered her into his arms while she cried. He held her until she pulled away.

She took in a breath and brushed her hair off her face. "I'm okay."

He touched her cheek with the back of his hand. "You sure?"

She nodded.

He hated destroying the tender moment between them. He rose to his feet, restarted the boat and headed toward an open area where he could get turned around. Lani came and stood beside him, squeezing his arm and then leaning against him so their shoulders touched.

It was over. Together, they'd defeated Martin. He'd be locked up, unable to torment anyone anymore.

He liked being this close to Lani. He only wished it could last.

* * *

Once Noah got the boat turned around, Lani watched as they drew closer to the shore of North Brother Island. It looked like the NYPD had gone all out to catch Martin. As they docked, she could hear men shouting at each other and dogs barking. One bark though was distinct. Even before they docked, she saw Scotty bounding toward them. Once they were on the pier, Noah and Lani gathered Scotty into their arms. Scotty licked Noah's face and then Lani's. "Boy, am I glad to see you."

Tony was the first to arrive at the boat with Rusty. He radioed that Noah and Lani had Martin in their custody. A swarm of other officers showed up to haul him away. The rope was taken off Martin and he was handcuffed and led away.

Lani and Noah stood beside Tony while Scotty and Rusty sat at attention.

"So I imagine he's headed to the psych ward," said Lani.

"For starters," said Tony. "They will double lock the doors so he can't hurt you or Katie. Yeah, I saw that photo album he made…weird."

Lani crossed her arms. "I don't think I'm the object of his obsession anymore. I shattered that fantasy when he actually got to spend time with me."

"Well, we'll make sure he can't come near Katie. That guy will be locked up for a long time," Tony said before stalking over to where some of the police officers were gathered.

Lani collapsed on the shore and Noah sat beside her. "I imagine that boat needs to be taken in for evidence."

"I can take it in to dock and make sure the techs

know where to find it." Noah turned to face her. "That way I can give you a ride home in style."

"I'd like that," she said as a feeling she couldn't quite name permeated her awareness. After Noah let the others know what he was doing, he and Lani loaded Scotty onto the boat.

The sun was coming up as they made their way along the East River past Rikers Island, the site of its namesake prison complex. Once they were docked and off the boat, Noah hailed a taxi. He held the door for her.

"For once, I don't have to escort you all the way to your door and make sure Reed is home."

"Not ever again," she said. Her words caused a sadness to flood through her. With Martin in custody, she and Noah would have no reason to work together so closely.

As they stood there facing each other with the sun warming her skin, she wished he would kiss her. It was an unrealistic longing, she knew, but all the same, it was what she wanted.

He touched her cheek lightly. "Get some sleep. We'll see you on duty later."

She nodded and got into the car. She stared through the window at Noah as he spoke on his phone. He probably had hours of work left to wrap up everything related to Martin. As the taxi pulled out onto the street, Lani swiped at her eyes where tears were forming.

She rested her head against the back of the seat letting the sadness wash through her.

NINETEEN

Noah paged through the website that featured pets for adoption, a website different from the Queens shelter website that they had been checking. Lani had suggested it weeks ago, when Oscar had been missing, as a method to find Snapper, Jordan's missing dog. With Martin in custody, Noah finally had a moment to do a search. He could have asked Sophie to do it, but he liked feeling like he was doing something to find Snapper.

They knew the dog was alive. Once in custody, Martin had confessed to Jordan's murder and admitted to keeping Snapper for a while. The psychologist who had conducted the intake interview with Martin assured them that whatever obsession Martin had had with Lani had been broken. Katie had become Martin's only focus.

Noah paged through the pictures. Almost all were mixed breeds or pit bulls. He stopped on a picture of a German shepherd. A double click provided more pictures and the story behind why the dog was available for adoption through a privately-run shelter.

The dog had been found wandering the streets. He was thin and dirty. The description said he had on a black collar, which is what Snapper wore. The shelter had cleaned him up. Noah clicked on the pictures hoping to see Snapper's markings. His heart stopped when a headshot of the dog showed the distinctive horizontal black lines that came out from each of his eyes. This had to be Snapper.

Noah picked up the phone.

A woman with a chipper-sounding voice answered.

"I'm Chief Noah Jameson of the NYC K-9 Command Unit. I have some questions for you about one of the dogs you have on your website, the German shepherd with the dark lines by his eyes."

"You're not going to believe this, but he was adopted less than two hours ago. I handled the adoption myself."

Noah's heart sank. Though recovering Snapper would not bring his brother back, it would provide some healing for everyone affected by his death. "Can you give me the name of the person who adopted him?"

The woman did not respond right away. Such information was probably somewhat private.

"I think that dog might be a highly trained missing police dog," Noah said.

"Oh, I understand. I can look up the information for you." He heard computer keys clicking. "We tried to detect a chip in the dog's shoulder but couldn't find one. It must have migrated. I'm so sorry we couldn't get him back to you. I have the information here on my screen." She read the name and address slowly.

Noah wrote down the information the woman gave him. When he looked up, Lani was standing in his doorway.

After Martin had been taken into custody, she'd requested three days off. Though it was what Noah would have suggested, it seemed a break in character for Lani.

She was all about working no matter what. She hadn't returned any of his texts in the three days she'd been gone.

Today she was dressed in jeans and a kimono-style jacket. She still wasn't ready for duty. With Martin finally locked away, he had assumed she would return to her training with a vengeance.

"You look like you've heard good news," she said.

"Maybe, I got a lead on where Snapper might be."

"That is good news." There was something about her that was different. "Look, I've been busy with...some things. Sorry I didn't return your texts. I was going to invite you out to coffee at Griffin's but when I went by there, there was a sign on the door. It looks like Lou has finally given up trying to keep the place open."

Noah put his hand over his heart. "That is a loss... a big loss."

The phone rang. Noah picked it up. "Chief Jameson."

"Noah, it's Tony. I just got a call. Martin overpowered a guard at the mental hospital and escaped. I'm with Katie right now. We think he might come after her. I'm making sure she's safe."

Noah's throat went dry and his chest felt like it was in a vise. "Any visual on him since his escape?"

"A patrol unit thought they spotted him back at Flushing Meadows. A BOLO has been issued and all patrol units are on alert."

"I'll head over there and have a look myself. This is personal at this point." He hung up the phone.

Lani took a step toward Noah. "It's Martin, isn't it? He's escaped. I'm going with you and Scotty. Let's finish this."

"You're not in uniform."

"You have an extra gun, don't you?"

Noah knew it was an act of futility to argue with her. He unlocked his drawer and pulled out his Glock. His own gun was nestled in the leather shoulder holster he had hung on the coat tree. He grabbed it and commanded Scotty to follow.

"We'll take my car," said Noah.

With Scotty trotting alongside them, Lani and Noah raced out of headquarters to the parking garage where Noah had his car. They drove through Queens to the park. He and Lani circled the park and then took Scotty out on foot patrol to question people. Several people had seen a man matching Martin's description.

After searching for another hour, they turned up nothing. Noah and Lani stood in the parking lot by his car.

Lani pointed toward a high-rise that was under construction. "I thought I saw a shadow in one of the windows." It was Sunday, so no construction workers were around. "People tend to go toward places they are familiar with."

Noah studied the dark building. "You think he's hiding out in there?"

"He's got to know there is an all-points bulletin out for him. He's probably laying low until the heat is off," she said.

Noah shrugged. "It's worth a shot."

The building had three floors that looked like they were mostly complete and the fourth floor was only steel framing. The place was probably locked up. That didn't mean Martin hadn't found some way in.

There were signs posted on the fence that indicated which construction company was doing the building. Noah looked up their number and got a recording of where he could call in case of emergency. Noah phoned the number, identified himself and got permission to enter the premises.

"If Martin is hiding in here, he didn't get through that locked door. He must have snuck in." They circled the building with Scotty until they found a part of the fence that had been cut away.

It didn't mean Martin was there for sure. Anyone could have slipped in there to hide out for any number of nefarious reasons. The only lead they had was that the last place Martin was spotted was the park next to this building under construction.

Both of them had their weapons drawn as they circled the outside of the building and Scotty followed them. They found a ladder propped against the back of the building leading up to the second floor where a hole for a window had been cut but no glass was in the window.

"Like old times, huh?" said Noah. "Climbing around." So much had happened between them since the training exercise at Jamaica Bay and then climbing around the abandoned building chasing Martin.

Lani's expression seemed to darken. She shook her head and smiled. "We've been through a lot together." He had the feeling she wanted to say something more, but there was no time.

Noah stared up the ladder. "I'll go first." Just in case Martin was waiting for them. Entering the building this way was hardly from a position of strength. He called for backup before going up the ladder into a room that was framed but lacking drywall.

Lani's excited voice from down below reached him. Scotty barked. "I see him, Noah. I see him."

"What?" Noah poked his head out. Lani was already

running across the construction site toward a backhoe parked by the other heavy equipment, with Scotty right behind her.

Martin's head bobbed up and then back down in the cab of the backhoe.

Lani had drawn her weapon and was racing toward where Martin was hiding.

Noah swung his leg around to get down the ladder. The rumble of the backhoe starting up surrounded him. His heart stopped when he looked for where Lani was. She'd fallen into a hole that must have been covered with a tarp.

Dirt cascaded around Lani as she rolled over and stared up at the sky. The spitting and hum of the backhoe engine grew louder. Above her, Scotty ran back and forth barking.

She scrambled to find her gun and get to her feet. The hole was maybe seven feet deep, probably the start of a trench to lay some pipe that led to the building.

She clawed the dirt and struggled to get a foothold that would allow her to escape. She looked up to see the arm of the backhoe above her with a full bucket, lifting so it could release and open, dropping dirt on her. When that happened, she'd be buried.

She dug her fingers into the loose dirt and tried to climb.

Noah was above her. He shot at the backhoe which must have delayed Martin. He held his hand out to pull her free. She clamored to get on level ground even as the backhoe charged toward them. Noah pulled her to her feet just as the dirt filled the hole. Scotty turned and barked at the backhoe.

Martin turned the backhoe, so it was headed straight toward Scotty. The front windshield was shattered where Noah's bullet must have hit. The dog stood his ground and continued to bark.

Noah drew his gun and shot at the cab of the backhoe. Martin kept the machine running but came to a halt. Noah stalked toward the backhoe with his gun drawn commanding Scotty to back down. The first shot had shattered but not broken the glass in the cab.

Scotty let out one more threatening bark before falling in place beside Noah.

Lani raised her own gun to back up Noah.

Martin swung the machine around and lumbered toward the edge of the construction site. She fired a shot that didn't reach its target.

They raced after him as he crashed through the fence, flung the cab door open and jumped out. Martin bolted away with Lani, Noah and Scotty at his heels. Lani pushed harder to run faster, closing the distance between her and Martin. Up ahead was a street bustling with people and cars.

Martin stepped onto the sidewalk and raced across the street while the light was still red. Cars honked and brakes squealed. Out of breath, Lani reached the sidewalk and stared across the street.

Martin's head disappeared into the crowd.

Noah and Scotty caught up to her just as the walk sign flashed. They crossed the street searching the sidewalk for several blocks. No sign of Martin anywhere. Across the street, patrol officers were getting out of their cars. That must be their backup.

A heaviness like a weight on her chest caused Lani to sit down on a bench outside a shop. She continued to scan the sea of faces. Once again, Martin Fisher had eluded them. As if sensing her mood, Scotty pressed against her.

Hours ago, she had come into Noah's office to tell him what she had been doing on her days off. Lani had made a decision to apply for a transfer when she heard that a spot had opened up in a new K-9 unit starting up in Brooklyn. With a newer unit, there was a better chance she'd get a dog sooner.

One of the officers radioed that there still was no sign of Martin.

"I think he got away." Lani rested her elbows on her knees and placed her palms on her cheeks.

"At least you're not a target anymore. I don't think Martin will come after you now that he doesn't associate you with Katie anymore." Noah rose to his feet, placing his hands on his hips and staring out into the street. "I'm worried for Katie's safety though."

"It sounds like Tony is staying pretty close to her."

Now with Martin still on the loose, the moment to tell Noah about the transfer felt awkward.

Noah sat back down. He pointed toward a coffee kiosk. "Weren't you going to buy me a cup?"

"Won't be as good as Griffin's, but sure." Noah must have sensed something was up. They bought their coffee and carried it back to the park. More news came via the radio that Martin was still at large.

They walked through the park watching red, gold and rust colored leaves twirl through the air. Still stinging from the defeat of Martin being on the run, Lani could not find the right moment to tell him about her transfer.

The truth was that she was afraid of what his response might be. Yes, she'd applied for the transfer to get a dog sooner, but more than anything, she'd hoped that if Noah wasn't her direct supervisor he might be open to them being more than friends.

Noah tossed his empty coffee cup into a trash can. "I've got to get back to work."

He turned to face her.

She stepped over to the trash can and threw her cup away as well.

He put a finger beneath her chin to lift her head. "Something up?"

She took in a breath. "Noah, I requested a transfer."

He let his hand drop to his side. "A transfer? Out of state?"

She thought she detected fear in his voice.

"No, there was an opening in the new Brooklyn K-9 unit. There's a better chance of getting a dog sooner there. I'm tired of waiting for one here in Queens."

Noah had a stunned look on his face. "Don't you like working in Queens...with me?"

"Brooklyn isn't the moon. I'll still see you." What had she expected? That he would declare his love for her.

"Yeah, I hope so." He sounded hurt. "Well, come on, I'll give you a ride back to headquarters. I'm sure you'll say your goodbyes." He trudged toward the parking lot then turned to look at her. "I still have to approve the paperwork. It hasn't come across my desk yet. I'm sure you'll be around for a few more days." She detected the note of sadness in his voice.

"You will sign the paperwork?"

"Of course Lani. I wouldn't keep you from your dream," he said.

She stared at his back as he walked away. "Noah Jameson. Stop right where you are. Turn around and tell me what you're thinking." Fear made her throat go tight.

He had at one time admitted his attraction to her. Had he moved on emotionally already and gotten over her?

He stepped toward her and locked his eyes on her. A light breeze ruffled his brown hair. "Lani, I'm happy for you. I think the new unit will be a good career move."

"Really, that's all you're thinking."

"No, I was thinking this too." He gathered her into his arms. His mouth covered hers.

She wrapped her arms around his neck while he drew her close and deepened the kiss. As he pulled away, the world seemed to be spinning. He rested his hand on her cheek.

"Well, look at that. Lani Branson speechless." Amusement danced in his eyes.

As she stared into his eyes and relished the softness of his fingers on her face, she still could not find words to respond.

He leaned in and kissed her lips again and then drew her to his chest. She closed her eyes, listening to his heart thud.

He brushed his hand over her hair and kissed the top of her head. "Did you take the transfer…for this? So we could be together?"

She still could not find words. She lifted her head and nodded.

He picked her up and twirled her around. "You have made me so very happy." He set her down.

He beamed as he gazed down at her.

She reached up to rest her hand on his face, to brush her fingers through his hair at the temple. "I love being here with you in this moment."

"And I love you," he said.

He gathered her into his arms and hugged and kissed

her. Lani buried her face against Noah's neck, loving the warmth and the musky smell of his skin. Her heart flooded with good feelings, knowing that they could truly be together, getting to know each other as more than friends. She looked forward to many more real kisses from Noah.

* * * * *

If you enjoyed Courage Under Fire,
look for Tony and Katie's story, Sworn to Protect,
available next month and the rest of the
True Blue K-9 Unit series
from Love Inspired Suspense.

True Blue K-9 Unit:
These police officers fight for justice with the
help of their brave canine partners.

Dear Reader,

I hoped you enjoyed going on an adventure with Lani and Noah and, of course, Scotty. I love watching the way a romance unfolds between two very different people, but the best part of this book to me is writing about the police dogs. I used to think I was a cat person. I still love cats, but since Bart the border collie came into my life eight years ago, I have a deeper appreciation and love for dogs. We got Bart at the shelter when he was eight weeks old. He and his mom were found in an empty house, left behind by his owner. He gives me so much joy. He's so tuned in to my moods and always happy to see me when I come home. The reason I say in the dedication that he is the dog who saved my life is that after my husband died, the only thing that got me out of bed in the morning was him being at the side of the bed, looking at me with bulging eyes and whining that he had to go potty. It was enough to motivate me to face the day ahead. I like to think that we will be greeted and welcomed in heaven the same way our dogs greet us when we step into our homes, rejoicing over our presence, offering unconditional love and infinite affection.

Sharon Dunn

Get 4 FREE REWARDS!

We'll send you 2 FREE Books plus 2 FREE Mystery Gifts.

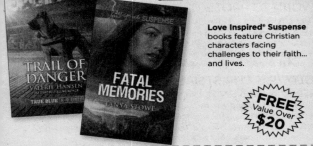

Love Inspired® Suspense books feature Christian characters facing challenges to their faith... and lives.

FREE Value Over $20

YES! Please send me 2 FREE Love Inspired® Suspense novels and my 2 FREE mystery gifts (gifts are worth about $10 retail). After receiving them, if I don't wish to receive any more books, I can return the shipping statement marked "cancel." If I don't cancel, I will receive 6 brand-new novels every month and be billed just $5.24 each for the regular-print edition or $5.99 each for the larger-print edition in the U.S., or $5.74 each for the regular-print edition or $6.24 each for the larger-print edition in Canada. That's a savings of at least 13% off the cover price. It's quite a bargain! Shipping and handling is just 50¢ per book in the U.S. and $1.25 per book in Canada.* I understand that accepting the 2 free books and gifts places me under no obligation to buy anything. I can always return a shipment and cancel at any time. The free books and gifts are mine to keep no matter what I decide.

Choose one: ☐ **Love Inspired® Suspense Regular-Print** (153/353 IDN GNWN) ☐ **Love Inspired® Suspense Larger-Print** (107/307 IDN GNWN)

Name (please print)

Address   Apt. #

City   State/Province   Zip/Postal Code

Mail to the **Reader Service:**
IN U.S.A.: P.O. Box 1341, Buffalo, NY 14240-8531
IN CANADA: P.O. Box 603, Fort Erie, Ontario L2A 5X3

Want to try 2 free books from another series? Call 1-800-873-8635 or visit www.ReaderService.com.

SPECIAL EXCERPT FROM

*An NYPD officer's widow becomes the target of
her husband's killer. Can her husband's best friend
and his K-9 partner keep her safe and take the
murderer down once and for all?*

Read on for a sneak preview of
Sworn to Protect *by Shirlee McCoy,*
the exciting conclusion to the
True Blue K-9 Unit series, available
November 2019 from Love Inspired Suspense.

"Come in," Katie Jameson called, bracing herself for the meeting with Dr. Ritter.

The door swung open and a man in a white lab coat stepped in, holding her chart close to his face.

Only, he was not the doctor she was expecting.

Dr. Ritter was in his early sixties with salt-and-pepper hair and enough extra weight to fill out his lab coat. The doctor who was moving toward her had dark hair and a muscular build. His scuffed shoes and baggy lab coat made her wonder if he were a resident at the hospital where she would be giving birth.

"Good morning," she said. She had been meeting with Dr. Ritter since the beginning of the pregnancy. He understood her feelings about the birth. Talking about the fact that Jordan wouldn't be around for his daughter's birth, her childhood, her life always brought her close to the tears she despised.

"Morning," he mumbled.

"Is Dr. Ritter running late?" she asked, uneasiness joining the unsettled feeling in the pit of her stomach.

"He won't be able to make it," the man said, lowering the charts and grinning.

She went cold with terror.

She knew the hazel eyes, the lopsided grin, the high forehead. "Martin," she stammered.

"Sorry it took me so long to get to you, sweetheart. I had to watch from a distance until I was certain we could be alone."

"Watch?"

"They wanted to keep me in the hospital, but our love is too strong to be denied. I escaped for you. For us." He lifted a hand, and if she had not jerked back, his fingers would have brushed her cheek.

He scowled. "Have they brainwashed you? Have they turned you against me?"

"You did that yourself when you murdered my husband," she responded.

Don't miss
Sworn to Protect *by Shirlee McCoy,*
available November 2019 wherever
Love Inspired® Suspense books and ebooks are sold.

www.LoveInspired.com

Cash remembered coming out to Ma Dixie's place at Christmas time growing up. The contrast with his own foster family's home had been extreme. There, six themed Christmas trees were spread throughout the house, decorated perfectly by the commercial operation that brought them out each year and took them away after the holidays. That same company had wrapped garlands around the staircase and strung lights outside the house.

It had all been grand. He remembered being shocked and impressed his first year with the family, because it had been so different from the humble holidays back in Alabama. But he hadn't been allowed to invite his brothers over; too much noise and mess, his foster mother had always said. If he wanted to see them, he had to find a ride out to Ma Dixie's, which he had done frequently.

Here, Christmas really felt like Christmas.

He opened another box of ornaments, pulled out an angel made of hard plastic and handed it to Holly to place on the tree.

"Is this your tree topper, Ma?" Holly asked, holding it up.

"Yes, it is. I usually have Pudge put it up, but...could you do it, Cash, honey?"

He did, easily reaching the top of the small tree. "Is Pudge okay?" he asked Ma. "Is that why the place isn't decorated yet? He's too sick to help?"

Ma arranged the last figures in the Nativity scene and sank down onto the couch. "That's part of it. Mostly, it's me feeling blue. I'm not used to Christmas with no kids around."

Holly tilted her head to one side. "Did you have a lot of kids?"

"Dozens," Ma said with a wide smile. "That's the beauty of being a foster parent."

"Oh," Holly said as she sank down onto an ottoman beside Ma. "Do you…not foster anymore?"

Ma sighed. "I really can't with Pudge having all these doctor appointments. I guess maybe we're getting too old for it." She looked wistfully at the tree. "I just, you know, always enjoyed having the little ones around."

Holly looked thoughtful. "Is that why you wanted to take care of Penny? Not to help me out, but to have a little one around?"

"That's part of it," Ma said, "but don't you worry about it. I understand being picky where your child is concerned."

"It's not pickiness," Holly said. "If I were being picky, who better than an experienced foster parent like you?" She reached out and rubbed Ma's arm back and forth, two or three times, an affectionate gesture that made Ma smile.

Cash came over and sat at Holly's side, leaning against the ottoman. His heart, like that of the Grinch in the movie playing muted on the television, seemed to be expanding.

He'd taken plenty of women to high-end Christmas parties and fancy restaurants. But sitting here in Ma Dixie's house, talking with her about holidays and kids and family problems, decorating the tree with her, felt different. Like coming home.

Like coming home, with Holly beside him.

He put that feeling together with the questions his brother and Pudge had been asking. He was getting the horrifying notion that he might be falling in love with Holly. But he wasn't the falling-in-love type, or the settling-down type. And Holly wasn't the type for a short, superficial fling.

So what exactly was he going to do with all these feelings?

Don't miss Lee Tobin McClain's
Low Country Christmas,
available October 2019 from HQN Books!

Love Inspired®

Discover wholesome and uplifting stories of faith, forgiveness and hope.

Join our social communities to connect with other readers who share your love!

Sign up for the Love Inspired newsletter at **LoveInspired.com** to be the first to find out about upcoming titles, special promotions and exclusive content.

CONNECT WITH US AT:

Facebook.com/groups/HarlequinConnection

 Facebook.com/LoveInspiredBooks

Twitter.com/LoveInspiredBks